HEARTS
UNBROKEN

BY MICHAEL ROJEWSKI

CHAPTER 1

Fated Glances

The bell above the door jingled softly as Eli stepped into the coffee shop, his frame barely disturbing the air, small, unassuming, and cautious. The rich aroma of roasted beans curled around him, mingling with the faint clink of cups and low murmur of conversation. He hesitated near the entrance, hands fidgeting with the brim of his hat, heart tapping a nervous rhythm in his chest. When he finally tugged the hat off, a halo of soft chestnut curls sprang free, refusing to lie flat and framing eyes the color of a summer sky. The hum of quiet conversations and the hiss of the espresso machine filled the air, but Eli felt a knot tighten in his stomach. At just five feet tall, he often felt even smaller in the vast, bustling world beyond the Amish community. The glow of laptop screens, the tangle of earbuds, and the casual laughter that drifted through the room only deepened his sense of being out of place. Places like this, with their easy familiarity and modern comforts, felt like stepping onto another planet—but still, something had drawn him here today.

He shuffled to the counter, his eyes darting nervously over the menu as though it were written in a foreign language—words like latte, cappuccino, and cold brew swimming before his eyes. So many choices, each more confusing than the last. His heart raced, fingers gripping the edge of his hat until his knuckles whitened. "Just coffee," he mumbled to the barista, barely audible over the clatter of cups and the hiss of the espresso machine. The young woman behind the counter offered a quick, polite smile, but Eli's gaze dropped to the floor before he could read anything more in her expression. As he turned with his drink, his gaze swept the room—and that's when he saw him again.

Matthew.

Matthew leaned back in his chair in the corner, his business suit immaculate, a notebook open in front of him. His dark hair was neatly combed, and a faint shadow of stubble softened the sharp lines of his jaw. At thirty-one, he carried himself with the quiet confidence of someone who had carved out his path, so different from the life Eli had always known. Eli's heart skipped a beat, warmth blooming in his chest, and before he could stop himself, a wide smile broke across his face.

Matthew's face lit up with recognition, a smile that instantly made Eli feel safe as he waved him over. The knot in Eli's stomach tightened, but this time it wasn't just nerves—it was something softer, almost hopeful, fluttering beneath the fear. With hesitant steps, Eli made his way to the table, clutching his coffee like a lifeline. Matthew shifted slightly, leaning back to give him space, his eyes warm and attentive, studying Eli as he fiddled nervously with his cup, fingers tracing the rim to steady himself.

At twenty-one, Eli seemed untouched by the kind of heartbreak Matthew had endured. There was something disarming about his innocence, a quiet sincerity that felt almost foreign to Matthew now. It was a stark contrast to the lies and half-truths that had unraveled his last relationship, leaving scars he still carried. Watching Eli now, Matthew felt a flicker of something unexpected— hope, perhaps, or simply the ease of being near someone so unguarded.

He thought back to those last weeks with his ex, the sickening realization that the person he had given a decade of his life to had been unfaithful, over and over again. Late-night absences, half-heard phone calls, the hollow look in familiar eyes—all pieces of a truth he couldn't ignore. The number of betrayals was a mystery he'd never uncover fully, and he wasn't sure he wanted to. Moving on had been the only option, yet the pain lingered, a shadow that curled at the edges of his thoughts, stubbornly refusing to fade.

"Espresso," Matthew said as Eli sat down, closing his notebook and leaning forward just slightly, eyes flickering with surprise. "I wasn't expecting to see you again."

Eli's fingers traced the edge of his cup, cheeks flushing as he glanced away, thoughts swirling just beneath the surface—hope, nerves, maybe even something like relief. "Me neither," he murmured softly, his voice barely above a whisper.

Matthew studied him, intrigued. At 5'8", he wasn't tall, but next to Eli's modest frame, the difference seemed to stretch with every inch of nervous energy between them. His thrifted clothes and quiet demeanor spoke of someone starting over, and there was something genuine in that— something raw and unguarded Matthew hadn't seen in years.

"What brings you to Willow Creek?" Matthew asked gently.

Eli hesitated, fingers fumbling with his cup, the words catching in his throat. "Just... starting over."

Matthew nodded slowly, the phrase stirring something familiar deep inside him. "Starting over is tough. But you'll figure it out. You've got time."

Eli smiled shyly, his eyes darting up to meet Matthew's for a fleeting moment before dropping back to his cup. His legs started to bounce slightly under the table—a quick, rhythmic motion that caught Matthew's attention. It was such an innocent, unintentional habit, but Matthew couldn't help but find it endearing, a small sign of the earnestness he hadn't realized he was longing for.

"You do that when you're excited, don't you?" Matthew asked, a teasing grin spreading across his face.

Eli froze, his bouncing legs coming to an abrupt halt as his cheeks flushed a deep pink. "I—I didn't even realize," he stammered, voice embarrassed and barely audible.

Matthew chuckled softly, leaning back in his chair, eyes warm. "Don't stop. I love it. It's... adorable."

Eli's heart fluttered at the compliment, a shy smile tugging at his lips as the café's soft murmur wrapped around them.

Eli's blush deepened, and he ducked his head, letting out a nervous laugh. "I—I-I don't think anyone's ever called me adorable before."

Matthew's eyes softened, and his voice was warm and sincere. "Well, you are. And it's one of those things that makes you... You."

Eli's smile lingered longer this time, a flicker of surprise melting into something quieter—acceptance, maybe even hope.

Eli looked up through his lashes, his shy smile creeping back as his legs began bouncing again—this time without hesitation. Matthew couldn't help but smile, watching Eli's nervous energy soften and brighten in his presence.

They started with the usual small talk—the weather, the charm of the town—but their conversation quickly deepened. Matthew learned about Eli's life in the Amish community, the world he had left behind, and the quiet courage it had taken to step into something so unfamiliar. Eli hadn't left because he stopped loving his community; he left because he finally loved himself enough to admit the truth—that he was gay. And in his world, that truth came with exile.

As Eli spoke, his voice faltered for a moment, eyes dropping to his hands. Matthew felt a swell of empathy, the weight of that loneliness settling between them.

"I didn't fit," Eli admitted quietly, voice trembling slightly as he traced a circle on the warm cup in his hands. "It's hard to explain. I love my family, and I love the life I had, but... there's this part of me that couldn't stay."

Matthew's expression softened, and he offered a reassuring smile. "Sometimes, you have to leave to find where you belong."

Eli looked up at him then, his smile shy but genuine, eyes bright with hope. "I guess," he murmured, a nervous laugh tucked beneath the words.

Matthew's tone softened, teasing but kind. "And how's that going so far?"

Eli laughed softly, ducking his head in that familiar way. "It's... scary. But meeting people like you makes it easier." His fingers tightened briefly around his cup.

Matthew felt a warmth spread through his chest, a smile tugging at his lips. "People like me?" he asked, curiosity and something softer mingling in his tone.

Eli glanced up, his smile widening. "Nice people."

For a moment, they simply looked at each other, the space between them humming with something unspoken but undeniable. Matthew leaned back, letting out a contented sigh as he watched Eli's legs bounce again—a small, simple sign of his growing comfort. To Matthew, it spoke volumes about the connection blossoming between them.

And for the first time in a long while, the loneliness in Matthew's heart felt a little lighter.

The Grocery Store Encounter

Eli had first seen Matthew at the local grocery store a week earlier. The fluorescent lights hummed softly overhead, mingling with the rustle of plastic bags and the faint scent of fresh produce. Eli had been nervously clutching a shopping list, his handwriting shaky as he scanned the aisles. At five feet tall, Eli often found himself looking up at people, and Matthew was no exception.

Their carts bumped softly, the clatter startling Eli.

"I'm so sorry," he stammered, cheeks flushing a deep red.

Matthew smiled—disarming and kind. "It's fine, really. Are you new in town?"

Eli nodded, words catching in his throat. He wasn't used to being noticed, much less spoken to by someone like Matthew—polished, confident, and completely at ease. The hum of the store seemed to fade for a moment, replaced by the quickening beat of his own heart.

Matthew's smile lingered before he nodded. "Well, welcome to Willow Creek. It's a good place to start fresh."

CHAPTER 2

Fragile Beginnings

A week after the coffee shop reunion, the days in Willow Creek passed slowly for Eli, each one blending into the next as he navigated the unfamiliar rhythms of his new life. The small room above the hardware store was bare and simple, the rough wooden floor creaking underfoot, and a thin shaft of afternoon light slipping through the dusty window. The bare walls stood as quiet reminders of everything he had left behind—and everything he still hoped to find.

The single window overlooked a narrow alley, offering little more than a sliver of sky framed by worn brick walls. The furniture—a narrow bed, a wooden chair, and a small desk—was functional but sparse. Though the first month's rent had been generously offered free by Mr. Higgins, the kindly store owner, the clock was ticking. With the end of his free month looming, Eli felt the weight of uncertainty pressing down. He needed work—any kind of income—or soon he'd be out on the street.

Most nights, Eli lay awake staring at the ceiling, his thoughts a tangled web of uncertainty and fear. He missed the familiar sounds of the Amish community—the creak of wooden floors, the soft hum of voices during evening prayer—but he also knew he could never go back. Not after leaving the way he did—not after telling them the truth about who he was. His hands clenched loosely at his sides as a slow breath escaped, a quiet reminder of the distance he had chosen to cross.

The mornings were quieter still, filled with the hum of the unfamiliar town and the occasional whistle of a distant train. Eli laced up his well-worn boots, the worn leather creaking softly,

and stepped out into the cool morning air. He wandered the streets of Willow Creek in search of something—anything—that might offer a flicker of belonging, a place to call home.

A Chance Encounter

One sunny afternoon, as Eli wandered near the town square, he spotted Matthew by a parked van outside the community center. The sight of him was grounding in a way Eli couldn't quite explain. Matthew's suit jacket was neatly folded over the passenger seat, and his shirt sleeves were rolled up to his elbows as he unloaded crates of wine. His movements were deliberate, efficient, yet unhurried. Though Matthew wasn't tall, Eli found himself tilting his head just to meet his eyes—a reminder of how small he truly was. The faint scent of oak barrels and fresh wine drifted through the air, mingling with the chatter of people nearby.

Matthew caught sight of Eli and smiled—a warm, genuine smile that made Eli's chest feel lighter. "Hey, Eli," he called, setting down a crate. "How's it going?"

Eli hesitated for a moment before stepping closer, hands stuffed nervously into the pockets of his worn second-hand jeans. "It's... okay," he said softly, voice barely above the afternoon hum of the town square.

Matthew gestured toward the crates. "Dropping off some wine for the festival next month. The community center is hosting a tasting event. Figured it was a good way to contribute." He gave a small, easy smile, eyes flicking toward the busy street.

Eli nodded, his gaze flickering to the crates. "You donate a lot to the town?"

Matthew chuckled, leaning casually against the van. "It's not just donations. It's about being part of something bigger. Willow Creek's my home, and I want it to thrive."

Eli felt a flicker of something hopeful stir within him as the sounds of the bustling town square drifted around them.

The way Matthew spoke about the town made Eli's chest ache with longing. He yearned to feel that kind of connection, to belong somewhere again. "That's... really thoughtful," Eli said quietly, a small, hopeful smile tugging at his lips as a gentle breeze stirred the leaves nearby.

Matthew shrugged, brushing his hands off on his pants. "It's no big deal. Speaking of the festival, you should come. It'll be fun—lots of good food, music, and plenty of wine."

Eli managed a small, tentative smile. "Maybe."

Across the square, two women sat at an outdoor café, their eyes narrowing as they watched Matthew and Eli talk. Claire and Jenny, Matthew's lifelong friends, had grown up with him and were fiercely protective, though even they couldn't deny the warmth in Eli's smile. Jenny leaned closer to Claire, whispering something with a worried frown, while the soft clinking of coffee cups mingled with the murmur of nearby conversations.

"Who's that?" Jenny asked, tilting her head.

"The new guy," Claire replied, taking a slow sip of her iced coffee. "I've seen him around. He's staying above the hardware store."

Jenny frowned, eyes narrowing. "He looks... harmless."

Claire's voice dropped, dark with past memories. "That's what we thought about Aaron." She glanced toward Matthew across the square. "Matthew's too nice for his own good."

The Community Center Meeting

Later that evening, Matthew invited Eli to sit in on a meeting at the community center. Eli hesitated at first, the low murmur of confident voices spilling from the open door making him doubt if he belonged among such articulate people. But something in Matthew's quiet encouragement gave him the courage to step inside and take a seat.

The meeting was lively, with Matthew at the center of it all. His charisma and leadership filled the room, his voice steady and authoritative as he spoke with thoughtful deliberation. He listened attentively, nodding along as others shared their ideas, the rustle of papers and low murmurs punctuating the discussion. Eli watched from the sidelines, admiration blooming quietly in his chest, both inspired and comforted by Matthew's presence.

Seated at the back, Eli's small frame felt even tinier among the towering personalities filling the room. The steady murmur of voices and shifting chairs underscored the confident presence around him—people who seemed to know exactly who they were and where they belonged. Eli, by contrast, felt like a shadow, barely noticeable. But every now and then, Matthew's eyes flickered to him, offering a brief smile or nod—a quiet reminder that he wasn't invisible. Eli straightened slightly in his chair, a flicker of reassurance warming his chest.

When the meeting ended, the room buzzed with conversation—laughter, overlapping voices, and the shuffle of feet—as people mingled and exchanged ideas. Eli lingered at the back, caught between wanting to stay and the urge to slip away. But Matthew sought him out, weaving through the crowd with practiced ease, a warm smile lighting his face as he approached.

"What'd you think?" Matthew asked, tone casual but curious.

Eli shrugged, managing a shy smile. "It was... different. But I can see why people listen to you."

Matthew chuckled, leaning casually against the wall beside him. "It's not as glamorous as it looks. Half the time, I'm just making things up as I go." He shot Eli a playful glance.

Eli laughed softly, the sound light and genuine. For a moment, his worries faded, replaced by the warmth of Matthew's presence.

"I'm glad you came," Matthew said after a pause. "I know it's not easy to put yourself out there."

Eli looked down at his hands, voice quiet enough to vanish in the air. "It's just…everything's so new. Sometimes I feel like I'm not… enough."

Matthew's expression softened. He placed a hand gently on Eli's shoulder. "You are enough, Eli. More than enough. Don't let anyone make you feel otherwise."

Eli looked up, blue eyes wide and vulnerable. "Thank you."

Matthew smiled, his hand lingering just a moment longer. "Anytime."

A Glimmer of Hope

As Eli walked back to his small apartment above the hardware store that night, Matthew's words replayed in his mind. The way Matthew believed in him—even when Eli struggled to believe in himself—was something he hadn't felt in a long time.

It was a small glimmer of hope. A fragile beginning, but a beginning nonetheless.

The cool night air whispered around him, carrying the faint scent of pine and distant town lights as Eli took a slow, steadying breath.

CHAPTER 3

A Step Closer

Every morning in Willow Creek began the same for Eli:
a quiet walk through empty streets and tangled
thoughts. Walking was second nature to him. Back in the
Amish community, it had been more than just transportation
—it was a time for reflection, a moment to find peace in the
steady rhythm of his footsteps.

At five feet tall, Eli was used to feeling small in a big
world. But here, in Willow Creek, he was trying to carve out
a space for himself. Each step through the unfamiliar town
carried the weight of uncertainty—and with it, the faint
hope of something better.

Crossroads in the Sunlight

That morning, as Matthew passed the café on his way
to a Business Alliance meeting, he spotted Eli. Eli's head
was bowed, shoulders hunched beneath the weight of his
worries, his expression distant and absorbed. The soft
murmur of the café and the scent of fresh coffee hung in the

air, but Eli seemed unaware. Matthew's brow furrowed with concern as he quickened his pace toward him.

"Eli," Matthew called out, his voice warm and inviting. Startled, Eli lifted his gaze—his pale blue eyes locking with Matthew's. For a moment, the noise of the morning faded, and a quiet understanding passed between them. Matthew's face softened into a reassuring smile, and Eli's tense shoulders relaxed ever so slightly.

"Good morning," Eli said softly, voice tentative but polite.

Matthew tilted his head, studying him with quiet concern. "You okay? You seem... distracted." He glanced briefly at the busy street, then back to Eli, his eyes gentle and patient.

Eli hesitated, then sighed, words tumbling out before he could stop them. "I need to find a job," he admitted, voice low and uncertain. "I only have a couple of weeks left before... I don't know what I'll do." He glanced down at his hands, fingers nervously twisting together.

Matthew nodded thoughtfully, his gaze steady. "Have you talked to many people around town?"

Eli shrugged, hands stuffed in the pockets of his jeans. "A few," he admitted. "But... I don't have any experience."

Matthew's lips quirked into an encouraging smile. "Come by the shop this afternoon. Let's see if we can come up with some ideas together."

Eli blinked, caught off guard by the offer. "Really?"

"Really," Matthew said with a reassuring nod. "We'll figure something out."

New Opportunities

That afternoon, Matthew kept his promise and sent Eli to meet Mr. Carpenter, the owner of a small landscaping business. The shop's modest storefront was surrounded by neatly arranged pots of flowers and shrubs, their scents mingling in the warm afternoon air. A faded "Help Wanted" sign had been in the paper for quite some time, and Eli hoped this might be his chance.

Mr. Carpenter was a burly man with a kind smile and an easygoing demeanor. He greeted Eli with a firm handshake and a welcoming nod.

Mr. Carpenter looked Eli over, his expression thoughtful. "Do you know much about landscaping?"

Eli shook his head, nerves evident in the slight tremble of his hands. "Not much, but I'm a fast learner. And I've done a lot of physical work before."

By the end of the conversation, Mr. Carpenter offered Eli a trial shift for the following week. As Eli walked back to Matthew's store, his eyes were wide with gratitude.

"Thank you," he murmured, voice barely above a whisper. Matthew smiled warmly, a reassuring presence beside him.

Matthew waved it off with a smile. "You don't have to repay me. Just do your best."

Eli nodded, his steps feeling a little lighter. For the first time since leaving the Amish community, he felt like he had a chance.

Inside Matthew's Reserve

A few days later, Matthew invited Eli to his wine shop to talk more about potential opportunities. When Eli stepped inside, he paused in the doorway, momentarily stunned by the elegance of the space. Shelves of dark, polished wood lined the walls, their rows of meticulously arranged bottles catching the warm glow from overhead fixtures. The air was cool and carried the faint, intoxicating scent of wine. Matthew stood near the counter, a welcoming smile on his face.

"This is incredible," Eli murmured, his eyes darting from the neatly labeled bottles to the polished marble counter. He took a hesitant step closer, fingers brushing the cool surface. "I've never seen anything like this."

Matthew smiled, leaning casually against the counter. His gaze swept across the rows of bottles, softening with quiet pride. "It's my second home. Took years to get it just the way I wanted."

As Eli admired the shop's intricate details, Matthew watched him, a faint smile tugging at his lips. He loved seeing someone appreciate what he'd built.

His wine business was thriving, but it was only one part of his life. The Business Alliance meetings, the nonprofit boards, the countless events he helped organize—those were what gave his success a deeper purpose.

"You've done so much," Eli said softly, his gaze drifting along the elegant shelves. His fingers brushed lightly against a bottle's label. "This place... It's incredible."

Matthew leaned back, his expression thoughtful. "I've been lucky," he said, glancing around the shop. "But it's not just about the business. It's about the community. Chairing the Willow Creek Business Alliance, working with local groups... it keeps me grounded."

Eli's eyes widened slightly. "You do all that?"

Matthew chuckled, nodding. "Yeah. I like knowing I can make a difference." His gaze drifted across the polished shelves. "Willow Creek's my home, and I want it to thrive."

Eli smiled shyly, his admiration evident. "That's... inspiring."

Matthew's gaze softened. "You'll find your way here, too," he said gently. "It takes time, but you'll get there."

For Eli, those words carried a weight that went beyond the moment. And for Matthew, seeing the spark of hope in Eli's eyes reminded him why he did what he did—why he worked to build a community where people like Eli could belong.

Matthew's Thoughts

Later that evening, Matthew walked through the quiet streets of Willow Creek, the cobblestones glowing softly under the streetlights. His hands tucked into his pockets, he breathed in the cool night air as his thoughts lingered on Eli. As chairman of the Business Alliance, Matthew's days were filled with meetings, events, and decisions that shaped the community. It was a role he took seriously—one that had earned him the respect of the town.

But tonight, his mind was elsewhere. He thought about the vulnerability in Eli's eyes, the shy way he'd smiled when Matthew offered his help.

He thought about how Eli's legs bounced excitedly whenever he got nervous or thrilled—a small, endearing habit that never failed to make Matthew smile.

For all the accolades and responsibilities that came with his position, Matthew rarely found moments of genuine connection.

Eli, with his quiet determination and unguarded demeanor, had stirred something in him he couldn't quite name.

The weight of the day melted away as he walked, a new sense of purpose settling in its place.

Matthew didn't know exactly where his path with Eli would lead. But he was willing to take the steps to find out.

CHAPTER 4

New Beginnings

The morning sun bathed Willow Creek in a warm glow as Eli walked toward the landscaping company where his trial shift awaited. His legs carried him forward, but his mind raced with uncertainty.

He gripped the frayed straps of his thrifted backpack—a small anchor against the weight of so much unknown.

Would he be good enough? Could he prove himself in a world so different from the one he left behind?

The questions looped endlessly in his head. He'd spent years mastering the tools and trades of the Amish community, but the modern world was a puzzle he was still trying to piece together.

First Impressions

The landscaping yard smelled of freshly cut grass and damp soil. Eli showed up early, nerves tight but determined to leave a good impression.

The owner, Mr. Carpenter, greeted him with a firm handshake, his grip steady and reassuring.

"Morning, Eli," Mr. Carpenter said, his weathered face creasing into a smile. "You ready to get your hands dirty?"

Eli nodded, his nerves tightening in his chest. He swallowed hard. "Yes, sir."

Mr. Carpenter handed him a pair of work gloves and gestured toward a truck loaded with bags of mulch and potted plants. "We've got a lot to do today. Stick with me, and I'll show you the ropes."

Eli followed him, his smaller frame dwarfed by towering piles of materials. Despite his nerves, the familiarity of physical labor began to ease his anxiety.

Hauling bags of mulch reminded him of carrying feed sacks on the farm, and planting flowers felt like tending to the garden back home.

Midway through the morning, Mr. Carpenter glanced at Eli, a knowing smile on his face.

"You're doing good, kid. Keep it up."

Eli's lips curved into a small, relieved smile.

Eli flushed with pride, barely resisting the instinct to bounce with excitement. "Thank you, sir."

A Visit from Matthew

Later that morning, a voice rang out from behind them.

"Well, look at you, hard at work."

Eli turned, startled, to see Matthew standing near the truck, his suit jacket folded neatly over his arm. The soft rustle of the fabric caught the morning breeze.

He carried himself with his usual effortless confidence, but the warmth in his smile immediately put Eli at ease.

"Matthew!" Eli said, his voice tinged with surprise and excitement. His legs bounced slightly as he stepped toward him. "What are you doing here?"

Before Eli could respond, Mr. Carpenter approached, extending a hand.

"Matthew Hawthorne. I recognize you from the Business Alliance—and, well, just about everywhere else," he added with a chuckle.

"You're on every billboard in town."

Matthew smiled, shaking Mr. Carpenter's hand.

Matthew laughed, shaking his hand firmly.

"Guilty as charged. And you must be Mr. Carpenter. I've seen you at meetings too. It's great to talk face-to-face finally."

"Likewise," Mr. Carpenter said. He gestured toward Eli. "This one's doing well so far. I'll see if I can keep him." Matthew glanced toward Eli, his tone turning fond.

"He's a gem. You'll be lucky to keep him. Eli's one of the hardest workers I've met."

Eli flushed, his legs bouncing again as he ducked his head. "Thank you," he murmured.

Self-Doubt

By the end of the day, Eli was exhausted. His muscles ached, and dirt clung to his clothes and skin, but there was a quiet satisfaction in the work he'd done.

Still, as he walked back to his room above the hardware store, doubts crept in.

Would Mr. Carpenter keep him on?

Was this job enough to support himself in the long run?

What if he failed?

He sat on the edge of his small bed, staring out the window as the town settled into the quiet of evening. For the first time in days, tears welled up in his eyes.

Leaving the Amish community had been the right choice, but the weight of starting over felt heavier than ever, pressing down on him with a quiet, relentless force.

An Unexpected Visitor

A knock at the door pulled Eli from his thoughts. He quickly wiped his eyes before opening it to find Matthew standing there, holding a bottle of wine in one hand and two elegant wine glasses, the shop's logo etched into the crystal catching the light.

The faint scent of wine drifted softly in the air.

"I figured you could use some company," Matthew said with a grin, stepping inside without waiting for an invitation.

Eli blinked, caught off guard, but a small smile tugged at his lips.

Startled and a little shy, Eli blinked.

"Wait, how did you know?"

"Mr. Higgins mentioned you'd had a long day," Matthew said, setting the bottle and glasses on the small table by the window.

"I thought a little wine and conversation might help."

Eli laughed softly, his legs bouncing slightly as he closed the door behind Matthew.

"You didn't have to do that," he said, though the warmth in his voice betrayed how much it meant to him.

Matthew poured the wine with a practiced hand, the dark liquid catching the soft light of the room.

"I wanted to," he said, setting the glass gently in front of Eli. "Now, tell me about your day."

Eli watched the swirl of wine in his glass, hesitating before answering.

Eli's Curiosity

As they talked, Eli confessed his unfamiliarity with alcohol.

"We didn't drink, obviously," he said, his voice carrying a mix of embarrassment and curiosity. His fingers traced the delicate stem. "I don't even know how to hold a wine glass properly."

Matthew's lips curved into a gentle smile.

Matthew chuckled, his voice warm. "Don't worry, you're in good hands."

Eli watched, almost mesmerized, as Matthew swirled the wine in his glass, the deep red liquid catching the soft light.

"You seem to know so much about it," Eli said, his tone tinged with quiet wonder. "How did you learn all this?"

Matthew smiled, leaning back in his chair.

"Before I opened the shop, I saved up for little trips— just a few weeks at a time. I'd travel to vineyards, taste wines, and talk to winemakers. I wanted to understand the story behind each bottle."

He paused, his gaze thoughtful. "Those experiences taught me more than any book ever could."

Eli listened intently, his blue eyes bright with curiosity.

Eli's eyes widened. "You traveled the world? That's... amazing."

"It was," Matthew said, his voice calm. "But the real challenge came later. I decided to become a Master Sommelier. It's one of the hardest titles to earn in the wine industry."

He paused, letting that sink in. "Fewer than twenty people in the world have passed the test on their first try."

A faint, almost self-conscious smile tugged at his lips. "I was one of them."

Eli's breath caught, his legs bouncing lightly under the table.

Eli stared at him, awe written across his face. "You must be a genius."

Matthew laughed softly, shaking his head. "Not a genius —just stubborn."

Eli's legs bounced under the table, his smile shy but wide.

Opals and Connections

As the evening wore on, Eli's natural curiosity began to shine. His voice lifted with quiet excitement as he shared, "They're my favorite gemstone," he said, his blue eyes brightening. "They're so small, but they're beautiful. The way they shimmer—it's like they're hiding something magical."

Matthew watched him closely, a gentle smile playing at the corners of his lips.

He noted the way Eli's legs bounced slightly as he spoke, his excitement barely contained. He's a tiny opal, Matthew thought. Beautiful, unique, and far stronger than he appears.

"You're like that, you know," Matthew said quietly.

Eli tilted his head, a small crease forming between his brows. "Like what?"

"Like an opal," Matthew replied softly.

"Small, but... stunning. And stronger than people think."

Eli blushed, his legs fidgeting wildly in a mix of bashfulness and disbelief. He looked down, a shy smile tugging at his lips.

"That's... the nicest thing anyone's ever said to me."

Matthew chuckled softly. "It's true."

For the first time that day, Eli felt a quiet sense of peace settle over him. He wasn't alone. With Matthew's support, he knew he could face whatever challenges lay ahead.

CHAPTER 5

Whispers and Shadows

The week ahead in Willow Creek passed in a whirlwind for Eli. Between trial shifts at the landscaping company and quiet evenings talking with Matthew, his days were fuller than he'd imagined. Yet beneath the surface, uncertainty lingered—questions about his future, his place in this new world, and what Matthew's kindness truly meant.

Though Eli was slowly adapting, the modern world still threw daily curveballs his way. On more than one occasion, Mr. Carpenter patiently explained basic concepts—how to use a debit card, the purpose of a work uniform—each time watching Eli's cheeks flush with quiet embarrassment. Yet his patience never wavered.

"Everyone starts somewhere, kid," Mr. Carpenter said one afternoon, clapping Eli on the shoulder with a warm grin. "You're learning fast. That's what matters."

Eli returned the smile, feeling a flicker of hope amid the uncertainty.

Eli carried Mr. Carpenter's words with him, but it was Matthew's quiet encouragement that buoyed his spirit the most. Their shared moments—whether in the cozy calm of Matthew's wine shop or over simple dinners—became a refuge, a safe haven in a world that still often felt too vast and overwhelming.

A Gathering at Matthew's Reserve

One Friday evening, Matthew invited Eli to an event at his wine shop—a small gathering to introduce new seasonal wines. It was meant to be a casual affair, but Matthew had insisted that he come. Eli felt a flutter of nerves at the thought, but also a quiet excitement he couldn't quite name.

"You'll get to meet some of the community," Matthew had said, his tone light but encouraging. "It'll be good for you."

Eli had hesitated, anxiety stirring in his chest—but the quiet warmth in Matthew's eyes had convinced him to say yes.

When Eli arrived, the shop was already buzzing with conversation. Elegant glasses clinked as guests sampled the carefully curated wines Matthew had chosen for the evening. Hovering near the edge of the room, Eli watched Matthew move effortlessly through the crowd, greeting everyone with the easy grace of someone who had long ago mastered the art of connection. A quiet mix of awe and nervousness fluttered in Eli's chest.

Eli couldn't help but marvel at him. The perfectly tailored suit seemed to wrap Matthew in quiet confidence, his laughter easy and genuine as he moved through the crowd. Standing there, dwarfed by the room's energy and poise, Eli repeated Matthew's words in his mind—"You belong here." His heart beat a little faster, holding on to that promise.

As Eli took a careful sip from the glass Matthew had poured, the smooth richness of the wine did little to calm the flush rising in his cheeks. Across the room, two women were watching him, their quiet whispers edged with curiosity—and something colder, like skepticism. Eli's grip tightened slightly on his glass as he hesitated, caught between the urge to slip away and the faint hope of being welcomed.

Claire and Jenny's Concern

Claire and Jenny stood near the counter, their glasses of wine untouched as their gazes stayed fixed on Eli.

"That's him, isn't it?" Jenny murmured, her tone edged with caution.

Claire nodded, her expression tight, arms folding across her chest. "That's the one. I've seen him with Matthew twice now."

Jenny sighed, swirling her glass without really seeing it. "He's… young. And nervous. I don't know, Claire. Do you think Matthew knows what he's doing?"

"That's the problem," Claire replied, her voice low. "Matthew always sees the best in people. But after everything with Aaron... I'm not sure he's thinking clearly."

Jenny glanced toward Matthew, now laughing with a group of guests. "He looks happy," she admitted softly. "Happier than I've seen him in years."

Claire's shoulders dropped a fraction, her expression softening. "Maybe. I just don't want to see him get hurt again."

The Interrogation

Later in the evening, Matthew brought Eli over to introduce him to Claire and Jenny. The exchange was polite, but Eli could feel the undercurrent of scrutiny in their gazes—a quiet measuring he couldn't quite escape. His chest tightened, and for a brief moment, he wondered if he truly belonged here.

"So, Eli," Claire began, her voice smooth but edged with quiet intent. She tilted her head slightly, eyes steady on him. "How long have you been in Willow Creek?"

Eli swallowed, his fingers tightening faintly around his glass before he answered.

"Not long," Eli replied, his voice steady even as a flutter of nerves stirred in his chest. "Just a few weeks."

"And what brought you here?" Jenny pressed gently, though her gaze narrowed as she studied him.

Eli's fingers brushed the rim of his glass, and for a heartbeat, his eyes flicked toward Matthew before answering.

Eli hesitated, stealing a quick glance at Matthew, who offered a quiet, encouraging nod. "I needed a fresh start," he said honestly, his voice soft and low. "I left the Amish community. It just... wasn't a good fit for me anymore."

Claire's eyebrow lifted, and she folded her arms lightly. "That must have been quite the adjustment."

"It was," Eli admitted softly, a small, determined smile tugging at the corners of his mouth. "But I'm figuring it out. Slowly."

The conversation continued, but Eli could feel the unspoken judgments hanging thick in the air. When Claire and Jenny finally excused themselves, he let out a slow, steady breath, feeling the tightness in his chest ease just a little.

Moments later, Matthew returned, an apologetic smile softening his features. "They can be intense," he said gently, placing a reassuring hand on Eli's shoulder. "But they mean well."

Eli nodded, though a shadow of doubt lingered in his eyes. "They don't like me, do they?"

Matthew sighed softly, his hand brushing reassuringly against Eli's arm. "They're just protective. Give them time."

A Late-Night Conversation

After the event ended and the shop had emptied, Matthew and Eli sat together in the quiet space, the air heavy with the scent of wine and polished wood. Eli's fingers traced lazy circles along the rim of his glass as his thoughts churned beneath the calm surface. "Your friends don't trust me," he said softly, the words barely above a whisper.

Matthew leaned back in his chair, his expression thoughtful. "They don't know you yet. But they will."

Eli hesitated, then asked quietly, "Do you trust me?"

Matthew's gaze softened. "I wouldn't have invited you here if I didn't."

The words hung between them, a quiet reassurance that eased the unease in Eli's chest. He returned a shy smile, his legs bouncing lightly beneath the table.

"Thank you. For everything."

Matthew chuckled softly. "You're welcome. And for the record, I think you handled Claire and Jenny pretty well. They've scared off more people than I can count." Eli laughed softly, the sound light and genuine. "I'll take that as a compliment."

A New Resolve

As the night wore on, Eli found himself opening up to Matthew like never before. He spoke of his fears, his hopes, and the persistent ache of not belonging—feelings that clung stubbornly despite his efforts. Matthew listened quietly, recognizing echoes of his own struggles in Eli's words.

"I know what it's like to feel out of place," Matthew said softly. "When I left my family's wealth behind, people thought I was crazy. But I needed to prove to myself I could make it on my own."

"You did," Eli said, admiration shining in his eyes.

"So will you," Matthew replied, his voice steady and sure.

"You're stronger than you think, Eli. And I'll be here to remind you of that whenever you need."

For the first time in years, Eli felt a flicker of something he hadn't dared to name: hope.

CHAPTER 6

The Complexity of Flavors

The soft hum of music filled Matthew's Reserve as Eli leaned on the counter, his gaze fixed on Matthew carefully pouring a glass of deep red wine. The elegant bottle bore a label in flowing Italian script. Matthew's movements were precise and practiced, each step showing his reverence for the craft he had mastered.

Lately, Eli had spent more evenings in the shop, helping Matthew with small tasks and soaking in the calm atmosphere. It felt safe here—a haven where the chaos of his new life quieted, and he could simply be himself.

"What are we trying tonight?" Eli asked, curiosity flickering in his voice.

Matthew smiled, setting the glass in front of Eli. "This is a Brunello di Montalcino. One of my favorites. Italian wines have a depth and elegance that's hard to match."

Eli picked up the glass hesitantly, his grip awkward. Though inexperienced with wine, he felt reassured by Matthew's patient guidance, who gently showed him the way.

"Swirl it lightly," Matthew instructed. "That helps open the aromas—lets the wine breathe."

Eli followed his lead, watching the dark liquid catch the light as it swirled. He sniffed cautiously, brow furrowing. "It smells... earthy?"

Matthew chuckled. "Good—that's the terroir. It's the essence of the place where the grapes were grown. Italian wines often carry hints of the soil, the air, even the weather of the region."

Eli took a small sip, eyes widening as the complex flavors unfolded on his tongue. "It's... different. Strong, but... bold in a good way."

"Brunello can be bold," Matthew said, his tone warm and encouraging. "But let it linger. Try to pick out the different layers—it's like a story unfolding on your palate."

Eli closed his eyes, concentrating. "It's... rich. Fruity, but there's something deeper underneath."

"Tobacco, maybe?" Matthew offered with a smile. "Or leather. Those are common notes in a Brunello."

Eli nodded slowly, a small smile tugging at his lips. "It's amazing. I never thought wine could be so... complex."

Matthew leaned against the counter, his expression thoughtful. "That's the beauty of it. Wine tells a story. Every sip is a piece of history—a glimpse into the land, the people who made it, the care they put into every bottle."

Eli looked at him, admiration shining in his eyes. "You make it sound like art."

"It is," Matthew said simply. "And the more you explore it, the more you realize just how much there is to learn."

Matthew's Journey

Eli tilted his head, curiosity brightening his eyes. "How did you learn all this? It's not something most people just happen to know."

Matthew chuckled, setting the bottle down gently. "It wasn't easy. Before I opened this shop, I didn't have much. I worked two jobs—bartending by night and delivering by day—just to save up for small trips. Whenever I could afford it, I'd visit vineyards, taste wines, and talk to winemakers. Those experiences taught me more than any class ever could."

Eli listened intently, his legs bouncing slightly with nervous energy as Matthew spoke.

"But that wasn't enough," Matthew added. "I wanted to dive deeper, to truly master the craft. That's when I decided to pursue the Master Sommelier title." "What's that?" Eli asked, leaning in with genuine curiosity.

Matthew's smile held a quiet pride. "It's one of the toughest certifications in the wine world. You need to master everything—tasting, pairing, service, and history. The exam is brutal; most people spend years preparing, and some never pass." "But you did," Eli said, awe clear in his voice.

Matthew nodded. "On my first try. Fewer than twenty people worldwide have ever managed that."

Eli's jaw dropped. "That's... incredible. You must be a genius."

Matthew laughed, shaking his head. "Not a genius. Just stubborn."

An Evening Out

Later that week, Matthew suggested they go out for dinner—a small celebration for Eli's first official week at the landscaping company. Eli had been hesitant at first, nervous about being out in public with Matthew, but Matthew's easy confidence soon put him at ease.

The restaurant Matthew chose was cozy and intimate, nestled in a quiet corner of Willow Creek's main street. The menu showcased rustic Italian dishes, and the wine list—naturally—was extensive. Matthew ordered a bottle of Chianti, sharing its rich history and importance in Italian winemaking, while Eli listened intently, his curiosity deepening with every word.

As the evening wore on, Eli found himself relaxing more and more. The wine, the food, and Matthew's easy company created a warmth that felt almost surreal. Eli laughed softly, his legs fidgeting beneath the table each time Matthew's smile reached his eyes.

A Moment of Connection

At one point, as Eli recounted a small victory from his workday, Matthew reached across the table, his hand brushing lightly against Eli's. The contact was brief—almost accidental—but it sent a jolt of electricity through them both.

Eli froze, his heart pounding as he met Matthew's gaze. For a moment, the bustling restaurant faded away. All Eli could feel was the warmth of Matthew's hand—its steady strength grounding him in a world that still felt unsteady.

Matthew hesitated, but instead of pulling away, he let his fingers linger, his thumb brushing gently against Eli's. A rush of emotions surged through him—an exhilarating yet vulnerable feeling, as if that simple touch had unlocked something he hadn't realized he'd been holding back.

Eli's breath hitched, his legs bouncing uncontrollably beneath the table. "Matthew..." he whispered, his voice barely audible.

Matthew offered a soft smile. "You don't need words," he said gently. "I feel it too."

The butterflies in their chests fluttered in unison, filling the space between them with something unspoken but deeply felt—a moment of pure connection, fragile yet unbreakable.

Aaron Returns

The tranquil moment was shattered as Matthew's expression suddenly froze, his gaze locking onto a figure across the room.

Eli followed Matthew's gaze, his stomach tightening as he spotted a man standing near the bar—sharp features, confident stance, and eyes fixed intently on Matthew. A flicker of something unreadable crossed the man's face before he started making his way toward their table.

"Matthew," the man said smoothly, a sharp edge lurking beneath his calm tone. "It's been a while."

Matthew's jaw clenched subtly, but his voice stayed steady. "Aaron."

Eli's heart sank. This is him—the ex.

Aaron's gaze shifted to Eli, eyes narrowing with a hint of suspicion. "And who might this be?"

Matthew straightened in his chair, his tone steady but firm. "This is Eli."

Aaron's smile was thin, his eyes cold. "Nice to meet you, Eli. Looks like Matthew's been keeping busy."

The comment was light, but the undertone cut sharper than the words themselves. Eli shifted uncomfortably, his legs bouncing slightly as he searched for something to say but found none.

"Why are you here, Aaron?" Matthew asked, his voice calm but edged with steel.

Aaron's lips curled into a smirk. "Just passing through. Thought I'd see how the other half lives."

Aaron shrugged, a forced casualness betraying the tension tightening his shoulders. "I was just passing through. Thought I'd stop by and say hello." He paused, his gaze flickering to Eli with a sharp, appraising edge. "You look... happy."

"I am," Matthew replied, his voice calm but edged with finality.

Aaron's smile wavered, a flicker of something— resentment, regret—passing over his face before he caught it. "Good for you," he said, quieter now.

He turned and walked away, leaving a heavy pause at the table that neither Matthew nor Eli filled right away.

The Aftermath

Eli looked at Matthew, worry tightening his small frame. "Are you okay?" he asked, his voice soft but steady.

Matthew exhaled, raking a hand through his hair. "I haven't seen him in years. Didn't think I ever would again."

"He seemed..." Eli's voice trailed off as his legs bounced under the table. "Angry?"

Matthew nodded, his gaze distant. "Aaron doesn't like seeing me move on. He lied to me for years, cheated more times than I can count—but somehow, he's the one who can't let go."

Eli reached across the table, his fingers curling around Matthew's. The touch felt bolder this time—a quiet reassurance he hoped Matthew would feel. "I'm sorry you had to go through that."

Matthew's gaze softened as he looked at Eli. "Don't be. That's behind me. What matters is now."

Eli offered a small, uncertain smile, his legs twitching under the table. "I really am glad you're happy."

"I am," Matthew replied, his tone steady. "And a lot of that is because of you." The words hung between them, unspoken emotions thickening the air. For the first time, Eli didn't just feel like part of Matthew's life—he felt like a reason for his happiness.

CHAPTER 7

Unspoken Desires

The evening air in Willow Creek was crisp as Matthew walked Eli back to his small room above the hardware store. Overhead, the stars glittered like scattered diamonds, their pale light brushing the quiet streets. They walked side by side, silence stretching between them, comfortable yet charged, an unspoken tension growing with every step.

Eli's mind raced, replaying the moment at dinner when Matthew's hand had brushed his. The memory of that touch still sparked on his skin, igniting a nervous energy he couldn't quite suppress. His legs bounced slightly as he walked. He glanced at Matthew, whose sharp features were softened by the moonlight, lost in thought.

"Thank you for tonight," Eli said softly, breaking the silence. "It was… special."

Matthew turned to him, a small smile playing on his lips. "You're welcome. I'm glad you came. I… enjoy spending time with you."

Eli felt his cheeks flush and quickly looked away, unsure how to respond. The butterflies in his chest had grown into a full swarm, their wings beating wildly as they reached the door to his room.

Crossing the Threshold

When they reached the top of the narrow staircase, Eli hesitated, his hand lingering on the doorknob. "Would you... Like to come in for a bit?" he asked softly, Quieter than candlelight's flicker.

Matthew paused, studying Eli for a moment before nodding gently. "I'd like that."

The room was small and simple, the furniture sparse but warm and lived-in. A single lamp cast a golden glow, softening the modest space. Eli hurried to clear a few stray items from the table, his movements quick and flustered. "Sorry, it's not much," he mumbled.

Matthew chuckled softly, his voice low and soothing. "It's perfect. Because it's you."

Eli froze for a moment, his heart skipping a beat at the sincerity in Matthew's voice. He turned to face him, their eyes locking in the quiet intimacy of the room. The air between them thickened, charged with something neither could ignore.

Matthew's gaze flickered downward briefly, noting how Eli's shirt hugged his lean, slightly toned frame. There was a quiet strength in the way Eli carried himself—small, uncertain, yet undeniably resilient. Matthew's eyes traced Eli's narrow waist, his thoughts momentarily unsettled by the pull he felt. It was a magnetic force he couldn't ignore.

A Shift in the Atmosphere

Matthew stepped closer, his movements slow and deliberate. "Eli," he said softly, "I don't want to overstep, but... tonight, when I touched your hand..."

Eli's breath caught. "I felt it too," he admitted, words spilling out in a rush. "I've never felt anything like that before."

Matthew's gaze held his, the intensity in his eyes making Eli's knees go weak. "Neither have I."

For a moment, neither of them moved. Then, as if drawn together by an unseen force, Matthew reached out, his hand brushing Eli's cheek. The touch was gentle, reverent—like he was afraid Eli might vanish if he wasn't careful.

Eli melted into the contact, his legs jittering with nerves. Matthew's thumb traced a soft line along Eli's cheekbone. "You're incredible, you know that?"

Eli shook his head, his voice trembling. "I'm not. I'm... just me."

Matthew whispered, his voice thick with emotion,

"And that's more than enough."

The First Kiss

The moment hung between them, fragile as a thin thread suspended in the air. Slowly, Matthew leaned in, his lips brushing against Eli's in a soft, tentative kiss—like a careful exploration of something new.

Eli's eyes drifted closed as he melted into the kiss, his fingers clutching Matthew's arms like a lifeline. The sensation was overwhelming—warmth and electricity coursing through him, igniting every nerve. His heart thundered in his chest, each beat ringing loud in his ears.

Matthew's hands found Eli's face, drawing him closer as the kiss deepened. His fingers brushed through Eli's soft, dark hair, and as they kissed, he felt the delicate curve of Eli's waist beneath his hands. Eli seemed fragile, yet beneath that delicacy was a quiet strength that stirred something fiercely protective in Matthew. Eli's hands slid up to Matthew's broad shoulders, his grip tightening as the kiss grew more urgent. The feel of those strong shoulders beneath his fingers made Eli's heart flutter wildly. For the first time, he felt truly desired—completely seen.

When they finally pulled apart, both were breathing heavily, their foreheads resting together. Matthew's hands stayed on Eli's waist, firm but gentle, his thumbs lightly tracing the fabric of Eli's shirt.

"That was..." Eli started, his voice trembling slightly.

"Perfect," Matthew said softly, a gentle smile spreading across his lips.

The Conversation That Follows

They sat on the edge of Eli's bed, the charged air between them now softened into a quiet calm. Matthew reached out and gently threaded his fingers through Eli's. He couldn't help but notice how small Eli's hand felt in his—delicate, yet steady.

"I need you to know something," Matthew said, his voice steady but serious. "I don't take this lightly. What I feel for you... It's real. And honestly, it's terrifying—because it's been so long since I let myself feel this way."

Eli glanced down at their joined hands, his thumb lightly tracing over Matthew's. "I feel it too. I don't fully understand it yet, but... I know it's real."

Matthew cupped Eli's face once more, his eyes locking onto his. "Then we don't have to rush. We'll take it one step at a time."

Eli nodded, a small, hesitant smile breaking through his nervousness. "Okay."

They spent the rest of the evening talking, sharing stories, and having quiet moments that felt more intimate than anything physical. As the hours slipped by, Eli leaned into Matthew, soothed by the steady rhythm of his breath—the calmest he'd felt in years.

An Unseen Watcher

As they sat together, a figure lingered in the shadows outside the window. Aaron stood there, his eyes fixed on the scene inside, his expression unreadable but taut with tension. His jaw clenched and fists tightened at his sides before he turned away, disappearing into the night, leaving only the faint echo of his footsteps behind.

CHAPTER 8

Ripples in the Water

The next morning, sunlight poured through the window of Eli's small room, casting a warm, golden glow over the quiet space. Eli stirred, his eyes fluttering open as he stretched. The events of the night before flooded his mind—their conversation, the kiss, the way Matthew's hands had lingered on his waist. A shy smile spread across his face, and his legs bounced slightly beneath the blanket, the memory filling him with a comforting warmth.

He sat up slowly, the weight of his new reality settling around him. For the first time in what felt like forever, he didn't feel entirely alone. Matthew's presence had brought a quiet sense of belonging—something Eli hadn't dared to hope for until now.

A Visit to Matthew's Reserve

Later that day, Eli made his way to Matthew's wine shop. The door chimed softly as he stepped inside, the familiar warmth of the space enveloping him like a comforting embrace. Matthew looked up from the counter, his face brightening the moment he saw Eli.

"Eli," Matthew greeted, his voice warm and bright. "What brings you here?"

Eli smiled shyly, fingers nervously twisting the strap of his bag. "I just... wanted to see you."

Matthew's expression softened, and he gestured invitingly. "You're always welcome here."

As they chatted, Matthew guided Eli through the shop's new arrivals, pulling bottles from the shelves and sharing their stories. Eli listened intently, curiosity sparking brighter with every detail.

"This one," Matthew said, holding up a bottle with a deep green label, "is a Nero d'Avola from Sicily. Bold, with dark fruit and spice, but softened enough to be approachable."

Eli tilted his head, eyes narrowing as he studied the label. "It sounds... complicated."

Matthew chuckled, setting the bottle down on the counter. "That's the beauty of wine. It can be as simple or as complex as you want it to be. It's about finding the ones that speak to you."

Eli hesitated before asking, "What's your favorite?" Matthew didn't have to think twice. "Italian wine, without a doubt. There's something about it—the way it balances tradition and innovation, the deep connection to the land. It's... soulful."

Eli smiled, admiration for Matthew growing with every word. "You love this, don't you?"

Matthew nodded, his eyes meeting Eli's. "I do. But it's not just the wine. It's sharing moments like this, talking, learning, connecting. That's what makes it worthwhile."

Eli felt a flutter in his chest, his legs bouncing slightly as Matthew spoke. "I like learning about it," he admitted, his voice soft but earnest. "It's... exciting."

Matthew reached out, his fingers brushing against Eli's as he picked up the bottle. The contact was fleeting, but it sent a familiar spark dancing between them. Eli's breath caught, his gaze dropping to where their hands had touched, and a warm flush crept up his cheeks.

Matthew noticed but didn't pull away. Instead, he let his hand linger just a moment longer, offering Eli a soft, knowing smile. The simple gesture made Eli's heart stutter in his chest, the warmth of that quiet connection spreading through him.

Paths Intertwined

As they stood by the counter, the bell over the door jingled softly. Matthew's smile faltered, his posture shifting almost imperceptibly. Eli turned to see why, and there was Aaron, stepping inside. His sharp features and self-assured stride cut through the cozy warmth of the shop, unsettling the quiet moment they'd shared.

"Aaron," Matthew said, his tone suddenly guarded.

Aaron's eyes flicked between Matthew and Eli, a faint smirk playing at his lips. "Matthew. Fancy seeing you here."

Matthew straightened, his posture shifting into something cooler, composed. "What do you want?"

Aaron shrugged, but his gaze settled on Eli a moment too long. "Just curious to see what's new... or who."

Eli's brows knit together. "Competition?" he echoed, unease twisting in his chest.

Matthew's jaw tightened; he stepped subtly in front of Eli, his posture protective. "Aaron, don't."

"What?" Aaron drawled, feigning innocence. His gaze swept over Eli, lingering deliberately. The smirk on his lips curled wider. "I mean, I get why you're so protective. Look at him—adorable in that... thrift store chic."

Eli stiffened, heat flooding his cheeks. Instinctively, he crossed his arms over his chest, trying to make himself smaller. Under Aaron's cold scrutiny, his half-step back felt like retreat—and only made him feel more exposed.

"Does he even own anything that isn't secondhand?" Aaron sneered, his tone dripping with condescension. "Or is this part of your charity work, Matthew?"

Matthew's expression darkened, his voice suddenly sharp. "That's enough, Aaron."

Aaron chuckled, leaning lazily against the doorframe. "I'm just saying. All these polished shelves, elegant bottles—and then, well... him. Doesn't exactly fit, does he?"

Eli opened his mouth, a flush creeping up his neck, but Matthew spoke first. His tone was ice-edged, every word deliberate. "You don't know anything about him. Eli has more strength, more resilience, and more heart than you ever did. And for the record, I think he looks perfect."

Aaron's smirk faltered, his bravado slipping just for a heartbeat before he straightened. "If you say so," he muttered. "Good luck with that."

The door jingled behind him as he left, and the tension seemed to drain from the room with his absence.

The Aftermath

Matthew turned to Eli, concern etched into his features. "Are you okay?"

Eli nodded, though his hands trembled slightly. "Yeah. I just... didn't expect that."

Matthew stepped closer, his hands settling firmly on Eli's waist, steadying them both. "I'm sorry, Eli. He's... part of my past I'd rather leave behind."

Eli looked up at him, vulnerability and confusion in his eyes. "Why does he care so much?"

Matthew exhaled, running a hand through his hair. "Because he knows how to hurt me. For years, I let him make me feel small. But now, seeing him try that with you... It's different. I don't care what he thinks anymore."

Eli's chest tightened at Matthew's words. He closed the space between them, leaning his slight frame against

Matthew's solid warmth. "Thank you," he whispered. "For standing up for me."

Matthew's expression softened, his thumbs brushing gentle circles at Eli's sides. "I'll always stand up for you. Always."

Eli's lips curved into a shy smile, his legs bouncing lightly with relief and affection. "Good," he murmured. "Because I'm not going anywhere."

Moving Forward

As the evening wore on, they sat together in the quiet shop, sharing a bottle of Matthew's favorite Chianti. Eli listened intently as Matthew recounted stories of vineyards, foreign cities, and the people who shaped his journey. In turn, Eli opened up about his own path—the fears he still carried and the dreams he was beginning to dare.

By the time stars twinkled outside the window, a rare peace settled over them both. Aaron's shadow still lingered, but it no longer felt insurmountable. Together, they were stronger.

CHAPTER 9

Heat and Shadows

Eli's second week at the landscaping company had been exhausting but fulfilling. Each day brought new challenges, and with Mr. Carpenter's steady guidance, Eli was slowly finding his footing. The unfamiliar rhythms of his new life no longer felt as overwhelming, and the evenings he spent with Matthew made the hard days worthwhile.

One such evening, Eli walked to Matthew's Reserve just after sunset. The golden light from the shop's windows spilled onto the cobblestone street, guiding him like a beacon. Inside, Matthew adjusted wine bottles, his rolled-up sleeves revealing strong forearms that sent a flutter through Eli.

The bell over the door chimed, and Matthew looked up, his face lighting up when he saw Eli. "You're here," he said, his voice warm, making Eli's chest tighten.

"I wanted to see you," Eli replied, cheeks flushing as he shifted nervously on his feet.

Matthew crossed the room in a few strides, stopping just in front of Eli. "I'm glad you did."

The space between them felt charged, like the air before a storm. Matthew's eyes lingered on Eli—his slight frame, his narrow waist, and the way his thrifted shirt clung to his toned upper body. He reached out, letting his fingers brush against Eli's hand, sending a ripple of electricity through them both.

An Unraveling

"Come here," Matthew murmured, his voice low and inviting. He led Eli to the back of the shop, where a small tasting area was tucked away from prying eyes.

In the softly lit corner, Matthew placed his hands on Eli's waist, pulling him closer. Eli's breath hitched, his legs bouncing slightly as he looked up at Matthew. The intensity in Matthew's gaze made his heart race.

"You drive me crazy, you know that?" Matthew whispered, his voice thick with emotion. "I can't stop thinking about you."

Eli's hands found Matthew's shoulders, fingers curling into the fabric of his shirt. "I... feel the same," he admitted, voice trembling.

Matthew leaned down, capturing Eli's lips in a slow, deliberate kiss. It was different from their first—a deeper, more confident claim, as though Matthew was staking a piece of Eli no one else had ever touched. Eli melted into it, his hands sliding up to Matthew's neck, pressing closer.

Matthew's hands roamed up Eli's sides, brushing over the toned contours of his upper body before settling back on his waist. "You're so beautiful," Matthew murmured against Eli's lips. "I don't think you even realize it."

Eli's cheeks flushed, legs bouncing again as he whispered, "I'm just... me."

"And that's more than enough," Matthew replied, voice steady and sure.

An Interruption

The bell above the door rang, snapping them apart mid-breath, their hearts still pounding. Matthew's forehead rested briefly against Eli's, his hands lingering on his waist.

"I should go see who that is," Matthew said reluctantly, frustration flickering in his voice.

Eli nodded, stepping back as Matthew straightened his shirt and headed toward the front of the shop.

Left alone in the tasting area, Eli's cheeks remained flushed, his heart still racing. After a moment, he noticed Matthew getting busy with a customer. Smiling shyly, Eli gave a small, friendly wave goodbye and quietly slipped out.

An Unexpected Encounter

The following day, Eli was alone in the landscaping yard, sorting through supplies, when a familiar voice made his stomach drop.

"Fancy seeing you here."

Eli turned to see Aaron leaning casually against the side of the shed, his smirk sharp and cold. "What do you want?" Eli asked, his voice steadier than he felt.

Aaron shrugged, eyes raking over Eli with thinly veiled disdain. "Just curious. What's someone like you doing with someone like Matthew? You're... not exactly his usual type."

Eli stiffened, crossing his arms tightly. "That's none of your business."

Aaron stepped closer, venom dripping from his tone. "You think you're special, don't you? Riding on Matthew's coattails, pretending you belong in his world."

Eli's fists clenched, his body trembling with barely contained rage. "You don't know anything about me."

Aaron laughed, cold and mocking. "Oh, I know enough. You're just a charity case—a project to make him feel good about himself. But let me give you some advice: Matthew gets bored easily. He'll move on, like he always does."

Before Eli could respond, a firm voice cut through the tension.

"That's enough."

Eli turned to see Mr. Carpenter striding toward them, his expression dark. "Aaron, I don't know what you're doing here, but you need to leave. Now."

Aaron's smirk faltered for a moment before he raised his hands in mock surrender. "Just having a friendly chat."

Mr. Carpenter stepped between them, his broad frame shielding Eli. "Doesn't look friendly to me. Get out."

Aaron glanced at Eli one last time, a smirk returning. "See you around."

Eli stared after him, knees weak as adrenaline faded. Mr. Carpenter's expression softened as he clapped Eli's shoulder firmly.

"You okay, kid?"

Eli nodded, voice wavering. "Yeah. Thanks."

"Don't let guys like that get to you," Mr. Carpenter said. "You're better than he'll ever be."

The Safe Harbor

That evening, Eli found himself back at Matthew's Reserve. As soon as he walked through the door, Matthew was there, his expression shifting from joy to concern when he saw the look on Eli's face.

"What happened?" Matthew asked, his hands immediately finding Eli's waist.

Eli hesitated, voice trembling as he recounted Aaron's words. Matthew listened intently, his grip tightening, anger flickering in his eyes.

"That's it," Matthew said firmly. "Aaron's done. I don't care what it takes—I'm going to make sure he stays away from you."

Eli looked up, eyes glistening. "You don't have to—"

"I do," Matthew interrupted, voice softening. "Because I care about you. No one gets to treat you like that."

Eli's legs bounced slightly as he leaned into Matthew, his small frame fitting perfectly against him. "Thank you," he whispered.

Matthew cupped his face, thumb brushing gently over Eli's cheek. "Always."

Their lips met again, slow and intense, as if Matthew was pouring every emotion into that single moment. Eli clung to him, hands gripping Matthew's shirt, the world fading away.

In Matthew's arms, Eli felt safe, protected in a way he hadn't been in years. For Matthew, holding Eli was like finding something he hadn't realized he'd been searching for: a connection that made everything else fall into place.

CHAPTER 10

The Introduction

The weekend arrived in Willow Creek with a gentle breeze and clear skies—the perfect backdrop for the outdoor café meeting Matthew had planned. For weeks, Claire and Jenny had been nudging him to introduce Eli, their curiosity about the mysterious young man growing with each passing day. Matthew had finally relented, though a pang of nervousness lingered as the day approached.

Eli, meanwhile, was a bundle of excitement and unease. The thought of meeting Matthew's closest friends twisted his stomach, but Matthew's soft touches and reassuring words eased the worst of his fears.

"They're going to love you," Matthew had said that morning, his hands resting gently on Eli's small waist as they stood by the door. "And if they don't, well—that's their problem."

Eli offered a shy smile, his legs twitching. "Thanks for always having my back."

"Always," Matthew whispered, leaning down to press a soft kiss to Eli's lips—a kiss that lingered just a little longer than expected, leaving them both flushed and breathless.

At the Café

The café buzzed with activity when they arrived, the air rich with the scent of fresh coffee and baked goods. Claire and Jenny were already seated at a small patio table, heads bent together in conversation. They looked up as Matthew and Eli approached, their smiles warm but their eyes sharp with curiosity.

"Matthew, Eli," Jenny greeted, her tone welcoming. "You two look great."

"Thanks," Matthew replied, pulling out a chair for Eli before sitting beside him. "Thought it'd be good to get together again—properly this time."

Claire smirked, her gaze flickering to Eli. "Hope we didn't scare you off the first time."

Eli shook his head, cheeks coloring. "Not at all—really nice to see you again."

The conversation started light, revolving around small-town news and updates. Eli was quiet at first, but as the woman asked about his work and interests, he began to open up. Matthew's hand occasionally found his under the table, squeezing gently—a silent reminder that he wasn't alone.

Claire's Skepticism

At one point, Claire leaned back in her chair, her gaze flickering between Eli and Matthew. "So," she began, playful but with a hint of curiosity, "how are things going between you two?"

Matthew chuckled, draping his arm casually over the back of Eli's chair. "Better than I ever could've hoped."

Eli smiled, warmed by the thought. "Matthew's been... more than amazing."

Jenny grinned. "We can see that. He's been different since you came into his life. Happier."

Claire raised an eyebrow, a smirk tugging at her lips. "Good. But you better keep it that way."

Their teasing eased the tension, and Eli found himself relaxing into the laughter. For the first time, he felt like he might actually belong in Matthew's world.

A Steamy Interlude

Later that evening, back at Matthew's cozy house, the light outside had softened to a warm, golden glow. Eli stood by the window, arms wrapped around himself as he gazed down at the quiet town below.

Matthew approached silently, his footsteps soft on the hardwood floor. He slid his arms around Eli's waist from behind, pulling him close. Eli let out a small gasp, instinctively leaning into Matthew's warmth, feeling the faint tremble beneath his touch.

"Today went well," Matthew murmured, his lips brushing against Eli's ear. "They like you."

Eli turned in his arms, hands resting on Matthew's chest. "You think so?"

"I know so," Matthew replied, his voice low and certain. "But it doesn't matter what they think. All that matters is how I feel about you."

Eli's heart raced as Matthew leaned down, capturing his lips in a slow, deliberate kiss. Their bodies pressed together, the heat between them building with every moment. Eli's hands slid up to Matthew's shoulders, grip tightening as a soft whimper escaped him.

Matthew guided them toward the couch, his hands exploring the toned lines of Eli's upper body as they kissed. His touch molded to Eli's narrow waist, their bodies pulsing together with growing intensity.

"Eli," Matthew whispered, pulling back just enough to meet Eli's gaze, his voice thick with emotion. "I know I say this a lot, but—you drive me crazy."

Eli's cheeks flushed, legs bouncing slightly as he whispered, "I feel the same."

Matthew smiled, his hands sliding up to cradle Eli's face. "Then let me show you how much you mean to me."

A Sudden Disruption

The peaceful moment was broken by the buzzing of Matthew's phone on the coffee table. He sighed, reluctantly pulling away to check it. His expression darkened as he read the message.

"What is it?" Eli asked, voice tinged with worry.

Matthew's jaw clenched. "Aaron."

Eli stiffened, legs bouncing nervously. "What does he want?"

Matthew set the phone down, his hand returning to Eli's waist. "It doesn't matter. He won't ruin this."

But Eli couldn't shake the unease settling in his chest. Aaron's shadow lingered—a quiet threat to their fragile happiness.

A Plan to Move Forward

As the evening stretched on, Matthew and Eli curled up together on the couch, the earlier tension melting into quiet conversation and stolen kisses. They spoke softly about the future—the life they hoped to build together—and for a while, the outside world felt miles away.

Yet even in these intimate moments, Aaron's shadow lingered. Though Matthew was determined to protect what they had, an uneasy truth settled in: their troubles with Aaron were far from over.

CHAPTER 11

Faith and Family

The morning sun peeked through the curtains of Eli's modest room, casting soft golden rays across the worn wooden floor. He sat on the edge of his bed, staring at the small wooden cross resting on the nightstand. It was the only object he had brought from his Amish life—a simple reminder of a faith he still held close, even as he struggled to reconcile it with the world he now inhabited.

This morning, Eli found himself lost in memories of his family—their faces, their voices flooding his mind. He missed them terribly: the warmth of his mother's love, the quiet strength of his father, the laughter of his siblings as they worked together on the farm. But each memory was tinged with pain, a sharp reminder of why he could never go back.

He had left abruptly, his decision made in the heat of despair. When he finally gathered the courage to come out as gay, the reaction was swift and devastating. His father's face had turned to stone before he hurled a chair across the room, shattering it. His mother's scream and tears mingled with heartbreak and confusion. The elders of the community had been called, and the verdict was unanimous: Eli was to be shunned.

The Weight of Meidung

In the Amish community, shunning—or Meidung—wasn't just punishment; it was a severing of ties. Eli had been cut off from his family, his church, his entire way of life. No letters, no visits, no acknowledgment of his existence. To them, he might as well have been dead. The thought made his chest ache—a hollow, gnawing pain that never fully faded.

But what hurt the most wasn't the loss of his home or even the routines he had known all his life. It was the isolation he felt even when he was with his family. Despite their physical closeness, Eli had always felt alone in their presence. They couldn't truly understand him, not fully. And no matter how hard he tried to suppress his feelings, they lingered like a secret wound refusing to heal.

In those moments of loneliness, Eli found solace in small, quiet acts. When the ache in his chest became unbearable, he would hug his pillow tightly at night, pretending it was someone who cared enough to hold him back. The act was strange, almost childish—but it was the only comfort he'd known.

Now, in those same moments, Eli reached instinctively for Matthew. Being in Matthew's arms, hugging him like that pillow, brought a peace he'd never experienced before.

It was no longer a hollow embrace, but one filled with warmth and understanding.

Finding Solace in Matthew

Later that evening, Eli found himself at Matthew's house, seeking the comfort he had come to depend on. Matthew greeted him with a warm smile, his hands immediately finding Eli's waist as he pulled him close.

"You've been quiet today," Matthew said gently, his eyes searching Eli's face. "What's on your mind?"

Eli hesitated, his voice barely above a whisper. "I miss my family."

Matthew's smile faded, replaced by an expression of understanding and concern. He guided Eli to the couch, sitting beside him and taking his hand. "Tell me about them,"

Eli spoke slowly, his words halting as he tried to explain the complexities of his Amish upbringing. He described the simplicity of their life, the closeness of their community, and the deep faith that permeated everything they did. But as he spoke, tears welled in his eyes.

"They'll never forgive me," he said, voice trembling. "Not for leaving, and definitely not for being... this."

Matthew squeezed his hand, voice steady. "Eli, you didn't do anything wrong. You were honest about who you are. That's something to be proud of, even if they can't see it."

Eli shook his head, tears falling freely now. Without a word, he shifted closer to Matthew, wrapping his arms tightly around him. It was the same way he had clung to his pillow those lonely nights in the Amish community, but this time, there was a steady heartbeat beneath his cheek and strong arms wrapped around him in return.

Matthew held him without hesitation, his hands moving gently across Eli's back. "You're not alone anymore," he murmured. "You don't have to carry this by yourself."

Shared Faith

When Eli's tears subsided, he sat back slightly, his hands still clutching Matthew's arms.

"You know, I grew up with faith being everything," he said quietly. "Even after leaving, I still believe. I don't know how to explain it, but... I know God is real. I know He's there."

Matthew's expression softened, a faint smile playing on his lips.

"I know exactly what you mean. I grew up in a Baptist family, and faith was the foundation of everything. It still is for me."

Eli's eyes widened slightly. "You believe in God?"

"Absolutely," Matthew replied. "I've questioned things over the years—who hasn't? But the one thing I've never doubted is His presence. And I believe He made us as we are for a reason."

Eli let out a shaky breath, the weight of his emotions making his legs bounce slightly.

"It's not something I hear often. Especially from... people like us."

Matthew chuckled softly, his hand brushing a strand of hair from Eli's face.

"No, it's not. But I think that makes it even more important. You and I? We're proof that faith and love can coexist. That we're not a mistake."

Eli's heart swelled at Matthew's words, his small frame leaning instinctively into Matthew's warmth.

"Do you really believe that?"

Matthew cupped Eli's face, his eyes filled with unwavering conviction.

"With all my heart."

A Steamy Moment

As their conversation deepened, so did the connection between them. Matthew leaned forward, pressing a tender kiss to Eli's forehead before trailing down to capture his lips, then his neck. The kiss was soft at first—a gentle reassurance that quickly grew more fervent. Their bodies pressed closer, a wave of heat surging between them, hearts pounding in unison.

Eli clung to Matthew, fingers gripping his shirt as the kiss deepened. Matthew's hands slid down to Eli's waist, pulling him nearer until their bodies throbbed with the intensity of their feelings. Hands trembling, Matthew slowly removed Eli's shirt. Eli returned the gesture, his own hands trembling as he pulled off Matthew's shirt. Then came pants, each movement charged with nervous excitement.

Matthew pulled back slightly, resting his forehead against Eli's. "You're incredible," he whispered, breath still catching. "Never forget that."

Eli's eyes shimmered, his voice barely a breath. "I don't feel alone when I'm with you."

Matthew smiled, hands brushing gently along Eli's sides. "You never will be."

Moving Forward

As the night wore on, they talked about their shared faith, their hopes, and the quiet fears that still lingered. For the first time, Eli felt he wasn't alone in his spiritual journey—that he had found someone who truly understood him.

In the hush of the evening, as they held each other close, both men recognized their bond for what it was: something rare and unshakable—a love built on trust, faith, and the courage to stay true to themselves. Matthew cradled Eli's cheek, his thumb brushing gently against his skin as he whispered, "You're my tiny opal."

Eli's eyes shimmered with emotion, his voice trembling yet certain. "I love you."

For a heartbeat, the world seemed to hold its breath. Matthew's heart surged, and a radiant smile lit his face, brighter than Eli had ever seen. Tears welled in Matthew's eyes, matching the drops that clung to Eli's lashes. He drew Eli closer, his voice thick with feeling. "I love you, too."

The words carried a profound weight—a shared acknowledgment of everything they had endured, and the quiet strength it had taken to arrive at this moment. It was a testament to the healing power of love. They held each other tightly, tears falling freely, not from sorrow, but from the overwhelming relief and beauty of finally being seen, finally being cherished.

In that moment, wrapped in the warmth of shared faith and the soft safety of Matthew's home, they knew they had found something extraordinary—something worth holding onto, and worth fighting for.

CHAPTER 12

A Safe Harbor

The days in Willow Creek had been kind to Eli lately. He had settled into a quiet rhythm at work, his evenings spent wrapped in the gentle warmth of Matthew's presence. Just recently, he'd paid his first month's rent to Mr. Higgins, who had offered the small room above the hardware store for one free month to help him get started. Holding that receipt in his hand had brought a flicker of pride—proof that, little by little, he was learning to stand on his own.

Each morning felt a bit lighter than the last, and Eli clung to those small victories. They felt like fragile affirmations that he could build something new, something steady, after so much upheaval.

But peace has a way of feeling temporary. And before long, Aaron's shadow crept back into Eli's life, unsettling the fragile calm he had worked so hard to create.

An Unsettling Encounter

It started with small things—glimpses of Aaron lingering near the places Eli frequented, always just out of view. But it escalated one evening as Eli walked home from work. The streetlights cast long shadows over the worn sidewalk, and when Eli turned a corner, Aaron stepped out from behind a parked car.

"Well, if it isn't Matthew's little project," Aaron sneered, his tone dripping with malice.

Eli's breath caught in his throat. "What do you want?"

Aaron took a step closer, the smirk never leaving his face. "You really think you belong in his world? You're nothing but a charity case—someone for him to fix. Do you honestly think he'll keep you around once he gets bored?"

Eli's legs trembled, his fists clenching at his sides. "You don't know anything about me."

"Oh, but I know enough," Aaron spat, his voice low and dangerous. "And I think it's time you left—before you ruin his life."

The threat hung heavy in the air as Aaron leaned in, his presence oppressive and suffocating. But before anything more could happen, a voice cut through the tension from across the street.

"Back off, Aaron!"

Both men turned to see Claire and Jenny striding toward them, their faces set with determination. Claire's voice was sharp, her finger pointed like a blade. "You're not going to intimidate him—not now, not ever. Leave him alone, or you'll regret it."

Jenny stepped protectively in front of Eli, her tone calm but resolute. "Go home, Aaron. You've caused enough damage."

Aaron's smirk faltered as he glanced between them, realizing he was outnumbered. With a muttered curse, he turned and stalked off into the night, the shadows swallowing him whole.

Eli let out a shaky breath, his legs threatening to give out beneath him. Jenny turned, her expression softening as she gently rested a hand on his arm. "Are you okay?"

Eli nodded, though his voice was barely a whisper. "Thank you."

Before he could say more, Claire wrapped her arms around him in a fierce hug. "You're part of Matthew's life, Eli—and that means you're part of ours. Don't let that creep make you feel otherwise."

For the first time that night, Eli felt the chill in his chest ease, replaced by the quiet warmth of belonging.

Matthew's Decision

That night, Eli told Matthew everything. He described Aaron's words, the cold fear that had gripped him, and how Claire and Jenny had come to his rescue. Matthew's jaw tightened as he listened, anger flashing in his dark eyes.

"You're not staying there anymore," Matthew said, his voice low but resolute. His hands came to rest firmly on Eli's shoulders. "That's it—you're moving in with me. Tonight."

Eli's eyes widened, his heart thudding in his chest. "Matthew, I can't. I don't want to be a burden."

"You're not a burden," Matthew insisted, his tone softening as he stepped closer. "I want you here because I love you. I want you close—where I can keep you safe."

Eli shook his head, tears welling up and spilling over. "I don't want you to feel like you have to take care of me. I'll cook, I'll clean, I'll—"

"Stop," Matthew whispered, pulling Eli against his chest. His voice grew gentler, wrapping around Eli like a promise. "You don't have to do anything. I don't want you here for what you can do for me. I want you here because you're you. Because I love you."

Eli clung to him, his small frame trembling as sobs shook his shoulders. "I love you too," he whispered, voice cracking with raw honesty. "I just... I don't know how to do this."

Matthew leaned back slightly, cupping Eli's tear-streaked face in his hands. His gaze was steady, warm, and full of quiet strength. "You don't have to do it alone," he murmured. "We'll figure it out together."

Moving In

The next day, Matthew and Eli packed up Eli's few belongings from the small room above the hardware store. It didn't take long—Eli didn't own much—but each item felt heavier than it looked, carrying pieces of his past and the quiet struggle it had taken to get here.

When they arrived at Matthew's house, Eli paused in the doorway, his breath catching. The space felt so different from anywhere he'd stayed before: warm, lived-in, and full of quiet details that spoke of someone who cared. It felt, impossibly, like home.

Matthew stepped beside him, his hand settling gently on Eli's narrow waist. Leaning closer, his voice dropped to a tender murmur. "Welcome home, Tiny Opal."

Eli blinked back tears, his heart swelling at the words. "Thank you," he whispered, his voice trembling with emotion. "For everything."

Matthew smiled softly and pressed a gentle kiss to Eli's temple. "Always," he whispered back, his thumb brushing soothingly against Eli's side.

For the first time in years, Eli let himself believe that maybe, just maybe, he truly belonged.

A Shared Future

That evening, as they settled into the rhythm of their new life together, Eli helped Matthew cook dinner. They moved easily around each other in the cozy kitchen, laughter rising over the soft clatter of utensils and the simmering sounds from the stove. It was simple, domestic—but to both of them, it felt profound: a quiet promise of the life they were building side by side.

Later, after the dishes were washed and the table cleared, they curled up together on the couch. Eli nestled against Matthew's side, his head resting on Matthew's chest, listening to the steady beat of his heart.

"I still want to contribute," Eli said softly, his voice muffled against Matthew's shirt. "I want to feel like I'm part of this—not just... taking."

Matthew's hand moved gently through Eli's hair, his touch slow and reassuring. "You're already part of this, Eli. You make this house feel like a home. That's worth more than anything else."

Eli looked up at him then, his eyes glistening with emotion. "I love you," he whispered.

Matthew leaned down, kissing him softly, the kiss lingering just long enough to say everything words couldn't. "I love you, too," he murmured against Eli's lips.

And as they held each other in the hush of the evening, surrounded by the soft lamplight and the quiet promise of tomorrow, they both knew: what they had built together was theirs, and no shadow from the past could ever truly take it away.

CHAPTER 13

Flames of Deception

Willow Creek had always been a quiet town, its nights filled with the soft hum of cicadas and the occasional rustle of leaves in the breeze. But on this particular night, that peace was shattered by the acrid scent of smoke and the ominous glow of flames rising from the heart of Main Street.

Eli stirred awake in Matthew's house, the faint sound of sirens cutting through the night. At first, it felt far away, almost dreamlike—but as the sirens grew louder, his heartbeat quickened.

Matthew was already up, phone in hand, confusion giving way to alarm as he stared out the window.

"Eli, get dressed. Something's happening downtown," Matthew said, his voice tense.

A Town in Shock

By the time they reached Main Street, a crowd had gathered. The hardware store—a pillar of the community for decades—was now swallowed by fire. The flames roared, wild and alive, their orange claws slashing at the night sky. Eli froze as the scene unfolded before him, his breath catching in his throat.

"That's... that's Mr. Higgins' store," he whispered, his voice trembling.

Matthew wrapped an arm around Eli's shoulders, pulling him close. "We'll find him. He's probably safe."

Firefighters battled the blaze with a sense of urgency, their silhouettes stark against the inferno. The heat was oppressive, even from a distance, and the crowd murmured anxiously as they watched the fire consume what had once been a symbol of stability and tradition.

Mr. Higgins stood near the edge of the crowd, his face pale and lined with worry. When he saw Matthew and Eli, he hurried toward them.

"Thank God you're okay," Higgins said, his voice shaking. His eyes lingered on Eli. "I thought you might have been up there."

Eli shook his head, tears welling in his eyes. "I wasn't... I wasn't there tonight. I'm so sorry, Mr. Higgins."

Higgins placed a hand on Eli's shoulder, his grip firm but reassuring. "Don't apologize, son. I'm just glad you're safe. That's all that matters."

The Morning After

By dawn, the fire had been extinguished, leaving the hardware store a smoldering ruin. The smell of charred wood lingered in the air as townsfolk gathered to survey the damage. Main Street, usually bustling with activity, felt eerily silent.

Matthew and Eli joined Claire and Jenny near the edge of the wreckage. Claire crossed her arms, her jaw tight. "This place has been here longer than most of us have been alive. It doesn't feel real."

Jenny nodded, her expression somber. "If Mr. Higgins hadn't had insurance, this would've been even worse. But still... something about this feels off."

Eli glanced at the blackened remains of the apartment above the store, his stomach twisting. "They'll investigate, right? To figure out what happened?"

"They better," Matthew said, his voice edged with steel. "Fires like this don't just happen."

The Investigation Begins

Within days, investigators combed through the wreckage, piecing together the story the ashes told. At the town meeting, the fire marshal's voice was heavy with weight.

"The cause of the fire has been determined to be arson," he announced. "Accelerants were used, and evidence suggests the fire was set intentionally."

Gasps rippled through the room, followed by murmurs of disbelief. For a town like Willow Creek, where everyone knew everyone, the idea of arson felt deeply personal.

Matthew's grip on Eli's hand grew firmer, his jaw locked tight. "This wasn't random," he whispered. "Whoever did this knew what they were doing."

Eli's mind raced, fragments of fear and unease swirling together. Aaron's face flashed in his memory—the sneer, the venom in his voice, the way he had lingered near the store just days before.

Unraveling the Truth

As the investigation progressed, subtle clues began to emerge. Surveillance footage from a nearby business showed a figure lingering near the hardware store late that night. Even grainy, the figure was unmistakable—broad-shouldered, striding with cocky ease.

Claire and Jenny were the first to confront Matthew and Eli with their suspicions.

"We saw Aaron near the store earlier this week," Claire said, her tone serious. "And let's not forget what he pulled with Eli."

Matthew nodded grimly. "It adds up. But we need more than that to prove it."

Jenny leaned in, her voice low. "I pulled a favor—someone at the sheriff's office is checking him out. They'll cross-check Aaron's whereabouts that night."

Eli, sitting quietly between them, felt a mix of gratitude and guilt. "If it was him," he said softly, "then he did this because of me."

Matthew turned to him, his expression fierce. "This is not your fault, Eli. He made this choice. He's the one responsible."

The Evidence Mounts

Days later, the sheriff's office confirmed the suspicions. Gasoline residue on Aaron's clothing matched the accelerants found at the scene. Witnesses recalled seeing him loitering near the hardware store earlier that evening. And finally, surveillance footage from a gas station showed him purchasing a can of fuel just hours before the fire.

The town was in an uproar. Aaron, once known for his charm, was now the subject of whispered accusations and outright condemnation. The sheriff announced that an arrest warrant had been issued, and Aaron was officially wanted for arson.

A New Beginning

The fire had left scars on Willow Creek, but it also brought the community closer. Townsfolk rallied around Mr. Higgins, offering support and donations to help rebuild. Matthew and Eli threw themselves into the effort, organizing fundraisers and spreading the word.

For Eli, the ordeal served as a reminder of both the darkness and the light in his new life. The shadows of his past—embodied in Aaron—still lingered, but they were no match for the love and strength he had found with Matthew and the community.

One evening, as they sat on the porch of Matthew's house, Eli turned to him, his expression thoughtful.

"I feel... safe here. For the first time in a long time."

Matthew smiled, wrapping an arm around Eli's shoulders. "That's all I want for you."

As they gazed out at the stars, the future felt brighter— a testament to their resilience and the bonds they had forged in the face of adversity.

CHAPTER 14

Shadows of the Past

The fire at the hardware store had shattered Willow Creek's calm. While Aaron's arrest brought some relief, it also left the town grappling with the painful knowledge that one of their own had committed such a heinous act. For Matthew and Eli, the event left an indelible mark—a lingering reminder of how quickly life could change.

Eli had moved fully into Matthew's house, but he still carried the heavy weight of guilt over the fire. Though Matthew had reassured him countless times that it wasn't his fault, the shadows cast by Aaron's actions clung tightly to him.

A Letter in the Night

One evening, as Matthew was preparing dinner, Eli heard the faint creak of the mailbox outside. He stepped onto the porch, expecting the usual stack of flyers and bills, but his hand froze when he saw an envelope with no return address.

The paper felt rough, and the handwriting on the front was uneven. Something about it sent a chill down his spine. He stepped back inside, his hands trembling as he handed the envelope to Matthew.

"This was in the mailbox," Eli said softly. "I... I don't know who it's from."

Matthew wiped his hands on a towel and took the letter, his expression darkening as he studied it. He opened it carefully, unfolding the single sheet of paper inside. The message was brief but chilling:

"You think you're safe? This isn't over."

Eli's breath caught in his throat. "Do you think it's from Aaron?"

Matthew's jaw tightened, and he placed a reassuring hand on Eli's shoulder. "He's in custody. He can't do anything. But I'll make sure the sheriff sees this."

Eli nodded, but the unease in his chest lingered.

Just a few days after the unsettling letter, another piece of shocking news rattled Willow Creek: Aaron had posted bail. Despite the severity of his charges, the legal system allowed him temporary freedom while awaiting trial. For the townsfolk, seeing him back on the streets was unsettling, but for Eli, it was terrifying.

Matthew was furious when he heard the news.

"It's ridiculous," he muttered, pacing the living room. "After everything he's done, they just let him walk around like nothing happened?"

Eli sat on the couch, his knees pulled to his chest. "Does this mean he can come near us?"

Matthew stopped pacing and knelt in front of him, his hands on Eli's shoulders. "No. The sheriff said there are strict conditions. He can't get near you, and if he does, he'll go right back to jail."

Eli nodded, but his unease was clear. The knowledge that Aaron was out there, watching, filled him with a sense of dread he couldn't shake.

Memories of the Amish Fires

Late at night, Eli lay awake in bed, staring at the ceiling. The glow of the hardware store fire was seared into his memory, its roar echoing like a ghostly whisper in his ears. The smell of smoke flooded his senses, dragging with it memories he had tried to bury—memories of fires in his Amish community.

Without phones or electricity, fire was a deadly, ever-present threat. He remembered the night the Miller family's barn had gone up in flames—the screams of the livestock, the frantic shouts of neighbors arriving too late to save anything.

He recalled the Anderson family, who had lost their three youngest children when their home caught fire while they slept. The fire department had been too far away to help in time, and the family's desperate cries had gone unanswered. The images of their charred home, the acrid smell of ash, had haunted him for years.

Eli turned onto his side, clutching the pillow tightly. His breathing was shallow, his chest tight. He knew he was safe in Matthew's house, but the fire had ignited an old fear—a fear that no matter how far he ran, the past would find a way to consume him.

A New Threat

The following day, Matthew took the letter to the sheriff's office, where it was carefully bagged as evidence. Sheriff Barnes, a seasoned officer with a no-nonsense demeanor, leaned back in his chair as he examined it.

"I'll look into it," Barnes said, his voice calm but firm. "But you both need to be cautious. Aaron might have friends—or accomplices-who-are-trying—are trying to intimidate you."

Matthew's brow furrowed. "You think the fire was just the beginning?"

Barnes shrugged. "It's possible. People like Aaron don't operate in a vacuum. Someone might have known what he was planning—or even encouraged it."

The thought sent a wave of anger through Matthew. "If anyone else is involved, I want to know."

A Familiar Face

As the investigation continued, Eli focused on settling into his new life with Matthew. He threw himself into cooking and cleaning, eager to feel useful and grounded.

One afternoon, while shopping for groceries, Eli noticed a familiar face near the produce aisle.

It was Aaron's younger brother, Daniel who worked at the store. Though Daniel had always seemed quieter and less confrontational than Aaron, his sudden presence sent a jolt of unease through Eli.

Daniel spotted him and approached, hands shoved into his pockets. "Eli," he said quietly. "Can we talk?"

Eli hesitated, glancing around the busy store. "I'm not sure there's anything to talk about."

Daniel sighed, his gaze dropping to the floor. "Look, I know what Aaron did was wrong—terrible, even. But I want you to know I had nothing to do with it."

Eli studied him carefully, searching for any sign of deceit. "Then why are you here?"

Daniel's voice dropped to a whisper. "I wanted to warn you. Aaron... he has friends. People who think like he does. They don't like what you represent."

He paused, glancing over his shoulder before adding, "Watch your back, Eli. They're not done."

Eli's heart raced as Daniel turned and melted back into the crowd. He hurried home, his mind swirling with the weight of Daniel's words.

Matthew's Promise

When Eli told Matthew what had happened, Matthew's reaction was immediate.

"That's it," he said, pacing the living room. "From now on, you're never going anywhere alone. I'll make sure someone's with you at all times."

Eli frowned, crossing his arms. "Matthew, I can't live in fear forever."

"You shouldn't have to," Matthew replied, his voice softening as he stepped closer. "But I won't risk losing you, Eli. Not after everything we've been through."

Eli sighed, leaning into Matthew's chest. "I just want this to be over."

Matthew wrapped his arms around Eli, holding him tightly. "We'll get through this. Together."

A Shocking Revelation

That night, as Matthew and Eli sat on the couch, Sheriff Barnes called. His voice was grave.

"We've got new evidence," he said. "The accelerants used in the fire were purchased under someone else's name. We think Aaron didn't act alone."

Matthew's grip tightened around the phone. "Do you know who?"

"We're narrowing it down," Barnes replied. "But I need you both to stay alert. This isn't just about Aaron anymore."

When the call ended, Matthew turned to Eli, his expression a fierce mix of anger and determination. "They picked the wrong people to mess with."

Eli nodded, fingers entwining with Matthew's. "I trust you."

A Shadow in the Night

Late that evening, as the town settled into a restless quiet, a lone figure lingered in the shadows outside Matthew's house. The faint glow of a cigarette briefly illuminated their face before they melted back into the darkness.

Inside, Matthew and Eli remained unaware of the watcher, their conversation drifting toward plans to rebuild and move forward. Yet the unseen presence was a chilling reminder: their battle wasn't over. The shadows of the past still stretched long across their future.

CHAPTER 15

A New Chapter

Willow Creek was beginning to find its footing again after the fire. Though the charred remains of the hardware store still stood as a stark reminder of what had happened, the town rallied around Mr. Higgins, determined to rebuild. Matthew and Eli were deeply involved, organizing fundraisers and pouring energy into community events to lift everyone's spirits.

Amid the bustle, Matthew decided it was time for Eli to meet Jenny and Claire on a deeper level. Though they had already played a protective role in Eli's life, Matthew wanted him to truly understand the bond they shared—and why their friendship meant so much to him.

Eli had never shared much about his past, but when Matthew mentioned the meeting, he finally opened up.

"I wasn't just different back home," Eli said quietly. "I was shunned. Not officially at first, but once they found out I was gay... everything changed. People stopped looking me in the eye. My family prayed louder. I had to leave before I vanished inside their silence."

Jenny and Claire: A Lifelong Bond

Jenny and Claire were inseparable—not just because they shared a small but cozy apartment on the other side of town, but because their lives had been intertwined for as long as they could remember. They had met Matthew in middle school, bonding over a shared love of movies and sarcastic humor. That friendship had carried them through the ups and downs of adolescence and beyond.

The three had grown up in a town about three hours from Willow Creek, a place Matthew rarely spoke about except with Jenny and Claire. It bordered the Finger Lakes, where Matthew had once worked at a quaint family winery. The peaceful rows of vines and shimmering lakes had offered him solace during his youth—a sanctuary from the pressures of growing up in a family that didn't fully understand him.

"The Finger Lakes were magical," Matthew had told Eli once. "I'd wake up early, watch the sunrise over the lake, and spend my days surrounded by the scent of grapes and oak barrels. It was the first place that felt like mine— where I could just be."

That experience had sparked Matthew's passion for wine and inspired him to create something of his own. Years later, he made that dream a reality in Willow Creek, opening four wine shops—all within a ten-mile radius—each carefully curated to reflect his vision. These stores served the tight-knit communities around town.

"I wanted each store to feel personal," Matthew explained one evening to Eli. "Not just a place to buy wine, but a place to learn about it. To experience it."

An Invitation

One evening, Matthew and Eli invited Jenny and Claire over for dinner. The air was rich with the aroma of roasted chicken and fresh herbs—a meal Eli had spent the afternoon preparing under Matthew's patient guidance.

"This smells amazing," Claire said as she stepped inside, her eyes lighting up when she saw Eli bustling around the kitchen. "Are you trying to show us up?"

Eli laughed nervously, cheeks flushing. "Matthew's the one who did most of the work."

Matthew shook his head, placing a hand on Eli's shoulder. "Don't let him fool you. He's a quick learner."

Jenny smirked as she settled into a chair. "I've got to say, Eli, you've done something pretty remarkable—you've managed to make Matthew happier than I've ever seen him."

Eli glanced at Matthew, his legs bouncing slightly as he smiled. "He's done the same for me."

Growing Knowledge

After dinner, the conversation shifted to Matthew's wine business. He spoke proudly about his four locations scattered around Willow Creek, each one designed to feel like a home for wine enthusiasts.

"Willow Creek may be small," Matthew said, "but people here appreciate a story in every bottle. That's what I try to give them."

Eli listened intently, his curiosity piqued. Over the past few months, Matthew had been teaching him about wine—the subtle nuances of flavor, the stories behind each bottle, and the care that went into crafting something so timeless.

Matthew turned to Eli, a small smile tugging at his lips. "Speaking of which, I've been meaning to ask—what do you think about leaving your landscaping job and working with me?"

Eli blinked in surprise. "You mean... at one of your stores?"

"Exactly," Matthew said. "You've got a knack for this, Eli. You've already learned so much, and I think you'd be amazing."

Eli hesitated, fingers fidgeting with the edge of his shirt. "I don't know... What if I mess it up?"

"You won't," Matthew said firmly. "And even if you do, that's part of learning. Besides, I'll be there to guide you."

Jenny and Claire exchanged a glance, their smiles growing. "I think it's a great idea," Jenny said. "You're already part of Matthew's world. This is just the next step."

A New Beginning

The following week, Eli officially joined Matthew's team. He started at the Willow Creek location, shadowing Matthew as he learned the ins and outs of the business. The transition wasn't without its challenges—deciphering wine labels in foreign languages, understanding the preferences of discerning customers—but Eli tackled each task with steady determination.

One afternoon, as they stocked shelves together, Matthew handed Eli a bottle of Barolo.

"This one," he said, "is what I'd call a thinking wine. It's bold, complex, and demands your attention. Not everyone appreciates it, but for the right person, it's unforgettable."

Eli studied the label, brow furrowing in concentration. "What makes it so special?"

Matthew smiled. "It's the way it's made. The grapes are grown in a specific region, harvested at just the right moment, and aged in oak barrels for years. Every step is deliberate. It's about patience and respect for the process."

Eli smiled gently, eyes meeting Matthew's. "Like us— slow and intentional."

Matthew's gaze softened as he placed a reassuring hand on Eli's back. "Exactly."

Lingering Shadows

Though Eli was finding his footing in this new chapter, the shadows of Aaron's actions hadn't completely faded. One evening, as he closed up the shop, a cold wind swept through the street, carrying with it the faint scent of smoke. Eli froze, his chest tightening as memories of the fire surged back like unwelcome ghosts.

When he arrived home, Matthew immediately noticed the tension in his posture.

"What's wrong?" Matthew asked softly.

Eli shook his head, voice barely above a whisper. "Sometimes... I feel like it's all going to happen again."

Matthew pulled him into a firm hug, his hands steadying Eli's trembling frame. "It won't. I promise, Eli. I'll do whatever it takes to keep you safe."

As they stood there, Matthew's phone buzzed on the counter. He glanced at the screen— a message from Sheriff Barnes:

"We need to talk. More evidence has surfaced."

Matthew's jaw tightened as he read the words aloud. "Looks like we're not done yet."

Eli looked up at him, fear flickering in his eyes. "What does that mean?"

Matthew cupped Eli's face, his gaze steady and firm. "It means we face it together. No matter what."

CHAPTER 16

Shadows Return, Light Prevails

The early autumn breeze carried the scent of fallen leaves and crisp air through Willow Creek. The town was slowly settling back into its steady rhythm after the chaos of the fire investigation, but an unspoken tension still lingered beneath the surface. For Eli, life had taken on a new kind of joy and purpose as he worked alongside Matthew in the wine shop. Yet, even amid these moments of happiness, shadows from the past threatened to reemerge.

Eli's New Confidence

Golden afternoon sunlight poured through the tall windows of Matthew's wine shop, casting warm rays across rows of meticulously arranged bottles. Behind the counter, Eli's small frame held a quiet but undeniable confidence as he spoke with a customer about a bottle of Burgundy.

"This one," Eli said carefully, cradling the bottle, "is from the Côte de Nuits region. It's known for its earthy undertones, with hints of cherry and—" He paused, searching for the word Matthew had taught him—"mushroom."

The customer raised an eyebrow. "Mushroom?"

Eli nodded, a smile tugging at his lips. "It might sound unusual, but it's part of what makes it unique. The soil in that area gives the grapes a very distinct character. It pairs beautifully with roast chicken or duck."

The customer glanced at the label again, curiosity overtaking skepticism. "You seem to know a lot about this."

Eli's cheeks flushed slightly, but his voice remained steady. "I'm still learning, but I've had a great teacher."

Matthew, watching from a few steps away, couldn't hide the proud grin spreading across his face. As the customer nodded in approval and added the bottle to their cart, Matthew stepped forward and clapped Eli on the back.

"You nailed it," Matthew said, his pride unmistakable. "I'm pretty sure you just sold them the most expensive bottle in the shop."

Eli blushed, his legs bouncing slightly with nervous excitement. "I just remembered what you told me about it."

Matthew leaned closer, his voice dropping to a playful whisper. "I think you've been holding out on me. You might be better at this than I am."

Eli laughed softly, shaking his head. "Not a chance."

Matthew watched Eli smoothly ring up the sale, his smile lingering. He had always believed in Eli's potential, but seeing it realized in such a tangible way filled him with a sense of pride he struggled to put into words.

Planning for Adventure

As the shop quieted down and the last customers trickled out, Matthew and Eli settled into the small tasting area, each with a glass of wine in hand. The soft afternoon light cast a warm glow over the bottles lining the shelves, creating a cozy bubble around them.

Matthew swirled his wine thoughtfully before looking at Eli with genuine admiration. "You've come so far, so fast," he said softly. "I think it's time we take your education to the next level."

Eli tilted his head, curiosity sparkling in his eyes. "What do you mean?"

Matthew's eyes lit up, excitement bubbling to the surface. "I mean travel. The best way to understand wine is to see where it comes from. To walk through the vineyards, meet the winemakers, and taste it right there—in the place it was born."

Eli's breath caught. "You mean... leave Willow Creek?"

Matthew nodded, reaching across the table to take Eli's hand gently in his own. "I want to take you to Italy, France, Spain—everywhere. Not just for the wine, but for us. To experience it all together."

Eli's face brightened, his legs bouncing with anticipation. "That sounds incredible, but… I've never even been on a plane."

Matthew chuckled, the warmth in his voice comforting. "Then it's about time, don't you think?"

Eli's eyes widened, a mix of excitement and nervousness shining through. "Do they serve food on planes? Do you eat it while flying?"

Matthew laughed, nearly spilling his wine. "Yes, Eli. They serve food. But honestly, I think you'll be too busy looking out the window to care."

Eli grinned, his enthusiasm infectious. "What if we get lost? Or end up in the wrong country?"

Matthew shook his head with a playful smile. "Then I guess we'll just make the best of it. But don't worry, I'll handle everything."

They clinked their glasses, the promise of new adventures stretching ahead like an open road, full of unknowns, but with the comfort of facing it together.

An Unexpected Laugh

As they mapped out potential destinations, Eli's face suddenly grew serious. "Will I need one of those… those things for traveling?"

Matthew blinked, caught off guard. "You mean a passport?"

Eli nodded earnestly. "Yes, that. How do I get one? Do you just tell someone where you want to go, and they write it down?"

Matthew burst out laughing, doubling over until tears streamed down his face. Eli stared at him, completely confused. "What's so funny?"

Between laughs, Matthew gasped, "You don't... You don't just tell someone and they 'write it down.'" He mimicked the gesture, cracking up all over again.

Eli crossed his arms, pouting. "Well, how was I supposed to know? We didn't need those in the Amish community."

Matthew wiped his eyes, leaning in to press a gentle kiss to Eli's forehead. "You're adorable, you know that? I'll help you get one. And I promise not to laugh... too much."

Eli smiled, shaking his head. "You're impossible."

Aaron's Return

As the day wound down and they locked up the shop, a sudden crash shattered the evening calm. Matthew spun around to see the shop's front window explode, shards of glass scattering across the pavement like jagged ice. Standing in the pale glow of the streetlights was Aaron, a smirk curling his lips.

"What the hell are you doing?" Matthew demanded, stepping instinctively in front of Eli, his stance protective.

Aaron's eyes gleamed with something wild and dangerous. "Just reminding you this place isn't for people like him."

Eli's heart thundered in his chest as Matthew closed the distance, voice low and cold. "You're done, Aaron. You've caused enough damage. Get out of here before I call the police."

Aaron's smirk twisted into a sneer. "This isn't over."

Without another word, he melted back into the shadows. Eli clung to Matthew's arm, voice barely steady. "What if he comes back?"

Matthew's arms wrapped around him tightly, voice steady and fierce. "He won't. Not if I have anything to say about it."

A Determined Step Forward

That night, Matthew called Sheriff Barnes to report the incident, his voice steady but seething with anger. The sheriff listened carefully and promised swift action. "He's violated the terms of his bail," Barnes said firmly. "I'll have him back in custody by morning."

The assurance brought a sense of relief, but the tension in the house was palpable. Later that evening, Matthew found Eli sitting on the couch, wrapped in a blanket, his knees pulled to his chest like a capitellum in a cocoon.

"Hey," Matthew said softly, sitting beside him. "You're safe with me."

Eli nodded, leaning into Matthew's side. "I just don't understand why he hates me so much."

Matthew cupped Eli's face, his gaze unwavering. "Because you're brave enough to be yourself. He sees the way I love you, and that terrifies him. But don't let his fear steal your light. You're stronger and more beautiful than he'll ever be."

Eli smiled faintly, his hand resting on Matthew's.

"I'm stronger because of you."

Matthew kissed him, their lips lingering as the tension of the day melted away.

"And I'm stronger because of you. I love you, my tiny opal."

Building Dreams

The next morning, Matthew received a call from Sheriff Barnes confirming that Aaron had been taken back into custody.

"He won't be causing you any more trouble," Barnes assured him.

The news brought a renewed sense of peace to Matthew and Eli's home.

Despite the day's events, Matthew and Eli threw themselves into planning their travels with fresh enthusiasm. They spent hours poring over winery guides, admiring pictures of rolling vineyards and historic cellars. For every shadow Aaron tried to cast, they responded with a step forward—a promise to keep building a life no one could take away.

That night, as they drifted to sleep wrapped in each other's arms, one truth was clear: their love was stronger than any fear, and together, they could face whatever came next.

CHAPTER 17

A Fragile Peace

The news of Aaron's return to custody spread quickly through Willow Creek, bringing a cautious sense of relief to the town. For many, it was a long-overdue step toward restoring the fragile safety they had all been craving.

For Matthew and Eli, it meant a chance—finally—to breathe again, to savor the quiet moments that had seemed impossible for so long. But beneath the calm, the scars of recent events remained raw. The memories of shattered glass and whispered threats lingered, shadows that stretched far beyond the locked doors of the past.

Though they moved forward together, the peace felt delicate, like a thin sheet of ice, beautiful but fragile, ready to crack at the slightest pressure.

Still, with each small victory and shared smile, Matthew and Eli held onto hope. They knew healing wouldn't come overnight, but their love was steady, a light strong enough to push back the darkness—even when it tried to creep in.

An Evening at the Shop

The wine shop buzzed with energy that evening as Matthew and Eli worked side by side. It was one of the store's busiest nights, with locals stopping in to grab bottles for dinner parties or to unwind after a long week. Eli had settled comfortably into his role, chatting easily with customers and confidently recommending wines.

A man approached the counter holding a bottle of Barolo, his tone uncertain. "I've heard this one is good, but I'm not sure how to pair it."

Eli's face lit up. "That's a great choice! It's bold and complex, so it pairs really well with rich dishes, like roast meats or a mushroom risotto." He hesitated for a moment, then added with a small smile, "Matthew always says wine should elevate the meal, not overpower it. He's been teaching me how to match wines with dinner, and now I can't imagine eating without thinking about what wine fits best."

The customer glanced between Eli and Matthew, as if trying to confirm something. His expression softened into a warm smile. "You two make a great team. And, if you don't mind me saying, a very cute couple."

Eli's cheeks flushed bright pink while Matthew chuckled from behind the counter, pride shining in his eyes. "Thank you," Matthew replied, light but sincere. "We like to think so, too."

The customer nodded, adding the bottle to his basket. "Well, keep up the good work. You're clearly doing something right."

Matthew leaned closer to Eli once the customer walked away. "You're incredible, you know that?"

Eli looked up, cheeks still tinged pink. "I just remember what you told me."

Matthew laughed softly. "That's the thing—you take it and make it your own."

A Special Request

Later that night, as they closed up the shop, Eli turned to Matthew with a thoughtful look in his eyes.

"Matthew, can I ask you something?"

Matthew smiled softly, securing the door behind them. "Of course. What's on your mind?"

Eli hesitated for a moment before speaking. "Would you take me to the wine country near where you grew up? You always talk about how beautiful it is, and I'd really love to see it for myself."

Matthew's eyes softened, a gentle nostalgia washing over him. "You mean the Finger Lakes?"

Eli nodded eagerly. "Yeah. The vineyard you worked at... the way you describe it, it sounds magical."

Matthew paused, then smiled warmly. "I'd love to take you there. It's been years since I've been back, but it's a place that's always stayed with me."

A Journey to the Finger Lakes

The next morning, they set out early, the crisp autumn air lending a refreshing clarity to the drive. As they neared the Finger Lakes region, the landscape shifted—rolling hills unfurled on either side, quilted with vineyards and dotted by quaint farms. Golden leaves shimmered on the surface of Cayuga Lake, reflecting the soft morning light like liquid amber.

Eli leaned forward in his seat, eyes wide with wonder. "It's even more beautiful than I imagined."

Matthew smiled, stealing a glance at him. "Just wait. The vineyard's even better."

They arrived at a secluded vineyard perched atop a gentle hill overlooking the shimmering lake below. Neat rows of grapevines stretched endlessly, their leaves turning fiery shades of orange and red. A light breeze carried the delicate scent of ripening grapes and wildflowers, while somewhere nearby, the soothing murmur of a waterfall added a serene soundtrack to the scene.

Matthew parked the car, and they stepped out together, the cool air brushing softly against their faces. Eli breathed deeply, his gaze sweeping across the horizon. "It's so peaceful here. I can see why you fell in love with this place."

Matthew nodded, pointing toward a narrow path winding through the vineyard. "Come on. I want to show you the spot where I used to take breaks. It was my favorite place in the world back then."

A Piece of Matthew's Past

They walked along the path, the soft crunch of fallen leaves beneath their feet blending with the distant rush of the small waterfall. Matthew led Eli to a quiet clearing next to the vineyard where a weathered bench rested beneath the sprawling branches of an ancient oak tree on a small cliff held back from a small chain-link fence. From this vantage point, the view stretched wide and clear—the lake's calm surface shimmering under the midday sun like a mirror.

"This is where I'd sit during breaks," Matthew said softly, his voice carrying a hint of nostalgia. "I'd watch the water, listen to the breeze, and think about what I wanted to do with my life. This place... it helped me find clarity. I even came back here when I found out about Aaron's infidelity and needed peace to gather my thoughts."

Eli settled beside him, eyes fixed on the tranquil waterfall that lead to the lake. "I can see why. It's like everything else just fades away here."

Matthew turned to look at him, his expression gentle and warm. "That's exactly how I felt. It's where I realized I wanted to build something meaningful—something people could come together to share and enjoy. That's what inspired me to open the wine shop."

Eli smiled, admiration blooming in his chest. "You've built something incredible. And now... I get to be a part of it."

Matthew reached out, intertwining their fingers with quiet certainty. "You're not just part of my life, Eli—you're the very best part."

Strengthening Their Bond

As the afternoon sun dipped lower, casting a warm golden glow over the vineyard, they wandered through rows of grapevines, tasting wines straight from the source and absorbing the stories Matthew shared about the craft. His passion was palpable, his eyes lighting up as he recounted memories from his time working here—the long hours, the delicate art of harvest, the patient wait for perfect ripeness.

Eli hung on every word, his curiosity igniting thoughtful questions that led them into deeper conversations —not just about wine, but about dreams, fears, and the lives they hoped to build together.

When they returned to the quiet clearing beneath the oak tree, a comfortable silence settled between them. Eli leaned his head against Matthew's shoulder, feeling the steady rhythm of his heartbeat.

"Thank you for bringing me here," Eli whispered, his voice soft with gratitude.

Matthew pressed a gentle kiss to Eli's hair. "Thank you for coming with me. Sharing this place with you... It means everything."

A Glimpse of the Future

As the sun slipped below the horizon, painting the lake in soft shades of orange and pink, they sat side by side in comfortable silence. The gentle roar of the waterfall blended with the rustling leaves, composing a peaceful symphony that wrapped around them.

Breaking the quiet, Eli's voice was thoughtful, almost tentative. "Do you think we'll ever have a place like this? Somewhere that's truly ours?"

Matthew's heart swelled with warmth. "I know we will. And it'll be even better—because we'll build it together, as us."

Eli met his gaze, hope shining bright in his eyes. "I'd like that."

As they stood and made their way back to the car, the vineyard slowly fading behind them, they carried more than memories. They held a promise—a future filled with love, discovery, and endless possibilities waiting just beyond the horizon.

CHAPTER 18

Meeting the Family

The journey to Matthew's parents' home was filled with quiet anticipation. The house, nestled in a charming suburb just outside the town Matthew grew up in, was the epitome of warmth and comfort. Matthew's parents, Eleanor and Robert, had always been welcoming and loving, but Matthew couldn't help feeling a pang of nervousness as he glanced at Eli beside him. This wasn't just any introduction —it was the beginning of a new chapter in their lives.

In the backseat, Jenny and Claire chatted quietly, their presence a deliberate choice by Matthew. He knew Eli would feel more at ease meeting his parents with familiar faces around, and the girls—ever protective of Matthew— were more than happy to help.

Breaking the Ice

The door swung open before they could even knock, Eleanor greeting them with a bright smile and open arms. "Matthew! It's so good to see you!" She hugged him tightly, then turned to Eli. "So you're the one I've heard so much about."

Eli offered a shy smile, his hand twitching nervously as he extended it. "It's nice to meet you, Mrs. Hawthorne."

Eleanor waved off the formality, pulling Eli into a warm hug. "None of that, Mrs. Hawthorne, nonsense. Call me Eleanor."

Robert, Matthew's dad appeared behind her, his tall frame filling the doorway. He extended a firm hand to Eli, his eyes kind but assessing. "Welcome, son. It's good to finally meet you."

Matthew watched the exchange with a mix of relief and affection. His parents were already making Eli feel at home, and he couldn't have asked for a better start.

Jenny and Claire stood behind Eli, and Eleanor turned to them with the same enthusiasm. "Girls, it's been too long! Come in, come in—all of you. Dinner's almost ready."

The warm, inviting smell of roasted chicken and fresh herbs greeted them as they stepped inside, the house a perfect blend of elegance and coziness. Eleanor had always prided herself on her ability to make anyone feel welcome, and tonight was no exception.

A Family Dinner

Dinner was a cozy affair, the table laden with Eleanor's home-cooked dishes. The soft glow of the chandelier overhead gave the room an intimate feel, and the clinking of cutlery and quiet conversation created a sense of ease.

As the conversation flowed, Eleanor and Robert asked Eli about his life, his interests, and how he'd ended up in Willow Creek.

Eli answered thoughtfully, his nerves gradually easing as he realized how genuinely interested they were in getting to know him. He spoke about his love for learning about wine and how much he had grown since meeting Matthew. He shared stories of working in the shop, his newfound confidence shining through.

"I have to say," Eleanor remarked, her eyes twinkling, "Matthew seems happier than I've seen him in years. And that's saying something."

Eli blushed, his gaze darting to Matthew, who reached under the table to squeeze his hand reassuringly. "I just... I want him to be happy, too."

Robert nodded approvingly. "That's all we've ever wanted for him."

Jenny, ever the observant one, chimed in with a grin. "He's come a long way, hasn't he? He went from juggling two jobs to running four wine shops—now look at him."

"Four shops?" Eleanor repeated, beaming with pride. "You didn't tell me you'd expanded again."

Matthew shrugged, his modesty intact despite his accomplishments. "It's nothing without the people who help me run it—including Eli."

The room filled with soft laughter, and Eli felt the last of his anxiety melt away.

A Private Conversation

After dinner, Matthew pulled Jenny and Claire aside while Eli helped Eleanor with dessert. The trio stepped out onto the porch, the cool night air wrapping around them. Matthew leaned against the railing, his hands gripping the edge as he hesitated.

"I've been thinking," Matthew said quietly, glancing at them, "I'm going to ask Eli to marry me."

Jenny's eyes widened, and a grin spread across her face. "Oh, Matthew, that's amazing!"

Claire leaned forward, her expression serious but supportive. "Are you sure you're ready for that? It hasn't been that long since... well, Aaron."

Matthew exhaled deeply. "That's the thing. With Aaron, I always felt like I was chasing something, trying to make it work even when it didn't. But with Eli, it's... easy. It feels right."

Jenny placed a hand on his arm. "Then do it. He loves you, Matthew. Anyone can see that."

Claire nodded, a small smile tugging at her lips. "And we'll help you make it perfect."

They talked in hushed tones about ideas for the proposal, Jenny and Claire tossing out playful suggestions while Matthew shook his head, laughing.

"I want it to be special," he said. "Something that feels like us."

Claire smiled warmly. "It will be. You'll know when the moment is right."

A Mother's Intuition

Later that evening, while Eli chatted with Jenny and Claire, Matthew found a quiet moment with his parents. Sitting in the living room, the soft glow of the fireplace illuminating their faces, Matthew hesitated before speaking.

"I wanted to tell you something," Matthew said softly. "I'm going to ask Eli to marry me."

Eleanor's face lit up, her hands flying to her chest. "Oh, Matthew, that's wonderful."

Robert leaned back, his gaze thoughtful. "I had a feeling you might be thinking about this. He's a good man, Matthew. Better than... well, you know."

Matthew nodded, understanding his father's unspoken words. "You didn't like Aaron."

Eleanor reached over, placing a hand on Matthew's. "We tolerated Aaron because we knew you loved him, but he was never right for you. We could see it, even if you couldn't."

Robert nodded. "Eli's different. He brings out the best in you. You smile more. You're... lighter."

Matthew smiled, his heart swelling with gratitude. "That's how I feel, too. And I want to spend the rest of my life with him."

Eleanor leaned over and kissed Matthew's cheek. "Then you have our full support. Always."

A Perfect Goodbye

As they prepared to leave, Eleanor pulled Eli into another warm hug. "You take care of our sweet boy, okay?"

Eli nodded, his voice quiet but steady. "I will. I promise."

Matthew watched the exchange, his heart full. He couldn't have asked for a better outcome. His parents adored Eli, and for the first time in a long time, Matthew felt a deep sense of peace about the future.

As they drove back to Willow Creek, Jenny and Claire dozed in the backseat, and Eli leaned against Matthew's shoulder, his breathing soft and steady. Matthew placed a gentle kiss on Eli's hair, whispering, "One day, I'll make you mine."

And as the miles disappeared beneath the tires, Matthew's mind raced with plans—not just for the proposal, but for the life they would build together, one filled with love, laughter, and the kind of happiness he'd always dreamed of.

CHAPTER 19

A Proposal in the Heart of Willow Creek

The idea had been lingering in Matthew's mind since the moment he met Eli. Standing alone in the wine shop, staring out at the quiet streets of Willow Creek, Matthew knew—it was time. Eli wasn't just a part of his life; he was the heart of it.

Matthew picked up his phone and called Jenny, knowing she would already be waiting for this moment.

"It's happening," Matthew said as soon as she answered.

"I told you!" Jenny exclaimed, her voice triumphant. "Claire, he's finally doing it!"

In the background, Matthew heard Claire mutter, "About time." Her voice came through the line louder as she added, "Alright, Matthew. Let's make this proposal unforgettable."

Rallying the Town

By the next morning, the plan was in motion. Matthew didn't have to explain much—Jenny and Claire were already organizing everything, from logistics to decorations.

"It has to be the coffee shop," Matthew insisted. "That's where it all began."

Jenny nodded. "We'll keep it simple and perfect. That's all Eli's ever wanted."

The owner of the coffee shop, Mrs. Reed, immediately offered to close the shop early that evening. "Matthew, after everything you've done for Willow Creek, it's the very least we can do. You've helped everyone here in some way. Let us do this for you."

The decorations were minimal but beautiful: soft fairy lights strung along the windows, a few small vases of fresh flowers on the tables, and candles providing a warm, romantic glow. The atmosphere was quiet and intimate, perfectly reflecting the simplicity and sincerity of their relationship.

Meanwhile, Matthew made a private trip to a jeweler in the neighboring town. He had been planning this for weeks, choosing a stunning men's engagement ring with an opal center stone surrounded by brilliant diamonds. It was elegant and one-of-a-kind, just like Eli: quietly beautiful and deeply meaningful.

The Big Day

The evening of the proposal, Matthew arrived at the coffee shop just as the sun dipped below the horizon, casting a golden glow across the town. The air was cool and crisp, carrying the faint scent of autumn leaves. Inside, soft light danced across the walls, creating a serene and magical warmth.

Eli arrived a little while later, escorted by Jenny and Claire under the pretense of grabbing coffee. As they stepped inside, Eli froze, his eyes widening as he took in the scene. Though dressed simply, Eli outshone everything in the room—Matthew had never seen him more radiant.

"What's... what's all this?" Eli asked, his voice barely above a whisper.

Matthew stepped forward, his heart pounding so hard it felt like it might burst. Butterflies danced in his stomach, and he could see the same nervous excitement mirrored in Eli's eyes. "It's for you," he said softly. "Because I love you."

Matthew reached out and took Eli's hand, the touch sending a shiver down both of them. "Do you know the very first time I saw you, I fell in love with your smile? It was the most beautiful thing I'd ever seen. And those blue eyes of yours... they made me melt. And they still do—every single day."

Eli's cheeks flushed, his legs bouncing slightly as his heart throbbed in his chest. "Matthew," he whispered, his voice trembling.

"You make me feel things I didn't think were possible," Matthew continued. "You understand me in ways no one else ever has, and I think… I hope… You feel the same."

Eli nodded, his eyes brimming with tears. "I do. I always have."

Jenny and Claire slipped quietly out of the room, leaving them alone. Matthew guided Eli to the center of the shop, where a small table held a single wine glass containing an opal—Eli's favorite gemstone. The last rays of sunlight faded beyond the horizon, leaving the room bathed in the warm glow of candlelight.

The Proposal

Matthew took a deep breath and dropped to one knee, his hand trembling slightly as he pulled the small box from his pocket. He opened it, revealing the opal engagement ring.

"Eli," Matthew began, his voice steady but full of emotion, "from the moment I met you, you changed my life. You've brought light into places I didn't even know were dark. You've shown me what it means to love deeply and fully."

Eli's eyes brimmed with tears as Matthew continued. "I don't just want to spend the rest of my life loving you—I need to. You're my tiny opal, my treasure, my everything."

Matthew held the ring up, the diamonds catching the candlelight. "Eli, will you marry me?"

Tears streamed down Eli's face as he nodded, his voice breaking. "Yes. Yes, I'll marry you."

Matthew stood, slipping the ring onto Eli's finger before pulling him into a kiss, soft, tender, and full of promises for the future. The warmth of the room seemed to envelop them, the world outside disappearing as they held each other close. Their hearts pounded in unison, the moment perfect in its simplicity.

Cheers erupted from a small crowd passing nearby, flooding the shop with joy.

A Quiet Celebration

After the proposal, Jenny and Claire returned with soft smiles, their quiet presence a comfort. They joined Matthew and Eli at a small table, sharing glasses of Matthew's finest wine as they celebrated together. There was no grand party, no loud fanfare—just the quiet joy of friendship and love.

Mrs. Reed stopped by briefly, her smile warm and bright. "Congratulations," she said. "You two deserve all the happiness in the world."

A New Chapter Begins

As they walked home later that evening, the cool night air wrapped gently around them. Eli couldn't stop staring at the ring on his finger. The opal caught the glow of the streetlamps, its iridescence mesmerizing.

"It's beautiful," he whispered. "You remembered."

Matthew smiled, sliding an arm around Eli's shoulders. "I remember everything about you."

Eli looked up, his voice soft. "I love you."

Matthew kissed him gently, his heart full. "And I love you. This is just the beginning, Eli. We have so much to look forward to."

Hand in hand, they walked through the quiet streets of Willow Creek, the promise of a bright future stretching out before them.

CHAPTER 20

Planning the Future

The days following Matthew's proposal were filled with excitement, anticipation, and the occasional swell of overwhelming emotion. The intimate moment had been perfect, but it was only the first step on their journey toward building a life together. Now, with their wedding on the horizon, the task of planning every detail became their focus —and with each step, the love between them grew even deeper.

Deciding on the Venue

One evening, Matthew and Eli sat in the cozy living room of Matthew's house, papers scattered across the coffee table. Matthew had lit a fire in the fireplace, the soft crackle of flames adding warmth to the room. They had been discussing ideas for the wedding, but Eli was quiet, staring at a blank page in his notebook.

Matthew tilted his head. "What's on your mind?"

Eli sighed, setting down his pen. "I just... I want it to feel special, you know? Not just for us, but for everyone who comes. I want them to see how much this means to us."

Matthew smiled, leaning over to take Eli's hand. "It will be special. You're making it special just by being you."

Eli's cheeks flushed, and he smiled shyly. "Do you have any ideas about where we should have it?"

Matthew hesitated, a soft smile spreading across his face. "Do you remember Briarwood Estate? The vineyard I took you to before the engagement?"

Eli's eyes lit up. "How could I forget? It was breathtaking."

Matthew nodded, his voice soft. "That's where I want us to get married. It's peaceful, beautiful, and full of memories for me. But it's not just about me—it's about us. When I saw you standing there by the waterfall, with the lake behind you, I knew. That's where we should start our forever."

Eli looked at him, his blue eyes glistening with emotion. "I thought the same thing when we were there. It feels... right."

With the venue decided, the excitement truly began. They marked a date in late spring, when the vineyard would be in full bloom and the air would be crisp but warm enough for an outdoor ceremony. Eli sketched ideas for decorations —simple, earthy tones to match the natural beauty of the setting—while Matthew worked on logistics.

Sharing the News

The next few weeks were a whirlwind of planning, but amid the flurry of activity, Eli found himself growing more introspective. One evening, as they sat together on the couch, Eli turned to Matthew, his expression thoughtful.

"Matthew, can I talk to you about something?"

Matthew immediately set down the wedding invitation draft he had been reviewing. "Of course. What's on your mind?"

Eli hesitated, fingers fidgeting with the edge of a blanket draped over his lap. "I've been thinking about my family. About how much I wish they could be part of this."

Matthew reached out, placing a comforting hand on Eli's knee. "Eli... I know how much they mean to you. And I know how hard it's been, being away from them."

Eli nodded, tears pooling in his eyes. "It's just... I don't even know if they'd want to come. But I feel like I need to try. I need to tell them about us, about how happy I am with you. Even if they don't approve, I want them to know."

Matthew leaned forward, cupping Eli's face in his hands. "Then let's tell them. We can write them a letter together—share everything you want to say. And if they don't respond, you'll still know you tried."

Eli's lip quivered as he leaned into Matthew's touch. "Thank you. For always understanding me."

The Letter

They spent the next few hours carefully crafting the letter. Eli poured his heart into every word, sharing his journey since leaving the Amish community, his fears, and how meeting Matthew had changed his life. He described their love, their wedding plans, and his hope that his family would accept the invitation to share in their happiness.

Matthew helped find the right words whenever Eli faltered, his steady presence a source of strength. By the time they finished, the letter was both delicate and heartfelt—a perfect reflection of Eli's sincerity.

As they sealed the envelope, Eli held it close to his chest. "I don't know if they'll come, but... I feel better knowing they'll know."

Matthew kissed his temple. "No matter what happens, you're not alone. We'll face it together."

Changes Among Friends

While wedding planning consumed much of their time, life continued evolving around them. One afternoon, Jenny and Claire invited Matthew and Eli to their shared apartment, faces glowing with excitement.

"We have news!" Jenny announced, practically bouncing on her feet. "I'm engaged!"

Matthew and Eli erupted into congratulations, hugging Jenny and admiring the elegant ring on her finger.

"That's amazing!" Eli exclaimed. "When's the wedding?"

Jenny laughed. "We haven't set a date yet, but I couldn't wait to tell you. Oh, and there's more—Claire's about to have the place to herself."

Claire smirked, leaning against the kitchen counter. "Jenny's moving in with her fiancé... but guess where? The apartment is right next door."

Matthew laughed. "So you're not exactly escaping each other."

Claire shrugged, her grin playful. "I'll take what I can get. At least now I can fill the entire apartment with my plants. Finally, some space for yoga without Jenny tripping over everything."

Jenny rolled her eyes. "You're welcome for keeping you sane all these years."

The banter continued, filling the room with laughter. Moments like these reminded Matthew and Eli how lucky they were to have such close friends by their side.

Anticipation of the Wedding and Honeymoon

As the weeks passed, the wedding plans came together seamlessly. Briarwood Estate was booked, and the cabins on the property were reserved for their honeymoon. They decided to stay for a week renting all four cabins so not to be interrupted, taking advantage of the vineyard's peaceful setting to unwind after the ceremony.

One night, as they lay in bed, Matthew described their honeymoon like a dream he'd been waiting to share.

"We'll walk through the vineyards at night when no one else is around. The stars will be above us, the lake shimmering in the moonlight."

Eli smiled, eyes closing as he imagined it.

"I can't wait to sit by the waterfall with you. We'll bring a blanket and wrap up overlooking the water. I'll curl into your lap to stay warm."

Matthew chuckled softly, brushing a strand of hair from Eli's forehead.

"Careful, sitting on my lap like that—you might heat us both up in more ways than one." His voice was low and teasing, lips curving into a mischievous smile.

Eli's cheeks flushed deep pink, and he laughed softly, swatting Matthew's chest.

"You're terrible."

Matthew caught Eli's hand, pressing a kiss to his knuckles.

"Terrible, but all yours," he whispered, eyes glowing with affection. "And I wouldn't have it any other way."

A Promise of What's to Come

As they finalized their plans, their love for each other grew even deeper. The vineyard, the ceremony, the life they were building—it all felt like a dream unfolding. And as they sealed the last of their invitations, they knew their journey together was just beginning.

CHAPTER 21

The Final Countdown

The days leading up to the wedding were a whirlwind of activity, emotions, and surprises. The small town of Willow Creek buzzed with excitement—nearly everyone knew about Matthew and Eli's upcoming nuptials. It wasn't just any wedding; it felt like a celebration for the entire community. The two men had touched so many lives, and now the town was ready to honor their love with the same generosity and warmth they had always shown to others.

The Letter's Response

One quiet morning, sunlight spilled through the kitchen window, illuminating the tidy counters and the faintly steaming mugs of coffee. Eli sat at the table, staring at an envelope in his hands. His fingers trembled slightly as he traced the familiar handwriting on the front—it was from his family.

Matthew stood nearby, leaning against the counter, his expression a careful balance of support and concern. He didn't press Eli, giving him the space he needed.

Finally, Eli broke the silence. "It's from my parents," he whispered, voice barely audible.

Matthew moved to sit across from him, resting his elbows on the table. "Do you want me here while you read it?"

Eli nodded, then carefully unfolded the letter. His eyes darted across the handwritten lines, his expression shifting from apprehension to a mix of relief and sadness. When he finished, he set the letter down, hands trembling.

"They're not coming to the wedding," Eli said quietly, his voice tinged with heartbreak. "They said they can't accept us... but they still love me. They hope I'll find happiness."

Matthew's heart ached for him. He moved to Eli's side and wrapped an arm around him, pulling him close. "I'm so sorry, love. I know you wanted more."

Eli leaned into him, resting his head on Matthew's shoulder. "It hurts, but... I think this is the best I could have hoped for. At least they didn't shut me out completely."

Matthew kissed the top of his head, holding him close. "You're not alone, Eli. You'll always have me. And tomorrow, you'll have a whole room full of people who adore you."

Eli's faint smile returned, Matthew's words easing the ache in his chest. "You're right. We have our own family now."

Last-Minute Chaos

Even with careful planning, the final week unraveled into chaos. Every time one issue was resolved, two more seemed to pop up.

One morning, Jenny burst into the wine shop where Matthew was organizing seating arrangements, phone in hand and panic written across her face. "The florist says they can't get the specific flowers you ordered—something about a shipping delay."

Matthew sighed, pinching the bridge of his nose. "Alright. Call them back and see if they can substitute with local blooms—something seasonal. If not, we'll just go with greenery."

Jenny smirked. "Rolling with the punches now? Who kidnapped perfectionist Matthew?"

Claire strolled in moments later, holding a revised guest list. "Speaking of perfectionists, we need to rework the seating chart. Your Aunt Margot refuses to sit next to Uncle Joe. Something about an argument over peach cobbler five years ago."

Matthew groaned. "This is why people elope," he muttered.

Eli appeared in the doorway, leaning casually against the frame. "You love this," he teased, blue eyes twinkling. "You love making everything perfect."

Matthew shot him a look of mock annoyance. "I love you, not this chaos."

Eli crossed the room and planted a quick kiss on Matthew's cheek. "You're doing an amazing job. It's going to be perfect because of you."

Jenny and Claire exchanged a knowing glance, their expressions softening. "And here we thought you were the romantic one, Eli," Claire teased.

The room erupted in laughter, the lighthearted moment melting away the tension.

A Quiet Escape

Three days before the wedding, Matthew and Eli decided to steal a few hours away from the chaos. They drove out to Briarwood Estate just as the sun began its descent, painting the vineyard in warm golden hues. The rows of grapevines stretched endlessly, their budding leaves glowing softly in the fading light. The lake shimmered in the distance—a vast expanse of blue cradled by rolling hills.

Matthew parked in the back of the estate near the waterfall, where chairs were already being arranged for the ceremony. The steady rush of the waterfall offered a peaceful counterpoint to the wedding frenzy. Eli stood still for a moment, taking it all in. "It's even more beautiful than I remember," he murmured.

Matthew slipped his arms around Eli from behind, resting his chin gently on his shoulder. "And soon, it'll be where we say 'I do.'"

Hand in hand, they wandered through the vineyard, a cool breeze carrying the faint scent of spring blossoms. At a small overlook with a clear view of the lake, Eli turned to face Matthew.

"Thank you," he said softly. "For giving me this. For giving me... us."

Matthew cupped Eli's face, his gaze full of love. "You're my world, Eli. This is only the beginning."

Their kiss was gentle, the world around them fading away as they held each other close.

An Unexpected Gift

The morning before the wedding, a knock at the door interrupted Matthew's meticulous review of his checklist. He opened it to find Mr. Carpenter standing there, holding a small wooden box.

"I wanted to give this to you," Mr. Carpenter said, his gruff voice softened by a rare tenderness. "It's nothing fancy, but I thought it might mean something to Eli."

Matthew carefully opened the box to reveal a handcrafted wooden plaque, engraved with the simple yet profound words: "Home is where love grows."

A genuine smile spread across Matthew's face, touched deeply by the gesture. "This is beautiful. Thank you."

Mr. Carpenter nodded, his eyes steady. "That boy's got a good heart. And you've got a good head on your shoulders. You'll take care of each other."

Matthew's voice was steady with conviction. "We will."

He tucked the plaque away safely, feeling the weight of the gift, not just the wood and words, but the unspoken acceptance behind them.

The Night Before

The evening before the wedding, Matthew and Eli welcomed a small, intimate gathering at their home. Jenny, Claire, and a handful of close friends filled the rooms with laughter and warmth. The comforting scent of freshly baked bread mingled with the rich notes of Matthew's favorite Italian wine, creating a cozy and inviting atmosphere.

Jenny raised her glass, her voice clear and full of affection. "To Matthew and Eli—the kind of love that makes you believe in magic."

Claire smirked, swirling her glass playfully. "And to Matthew's patience for Eli's adorable but slow wine education."

Eli blushed, cheeks tinged pink, while Matthew chuckled, pulling Eli close. "He's caught on faster than you think."

As the night unfolded, the conversation softened, shifting from playful teasing to shared memories and dreams for the future. When the last guest slipped out, the house settled into a serene quiet, wrapped in the peaceful glow that only comes from being surrounded by those who truly love you.

Under the Stars

Later that night, Matthew and Eli sat together on the porch swing, wrapped snugly in a thick blanket. The stars above shimmered brighter than usual, their soft light reflecting in Eli's eyes.

"Tomorrow," Eli whispered, his head resting against Matthew's chest, "we'll be married."

Matthew pressed a gentle kiss to the top of Eli's head, his voice full of quiet wonder. "I can't wait to call you my husband."

Eli smiled, fingers intertwining with Matthew's. "I've never been this happy. You've given me a life I never thought possible."

Matthew tightened his embrace, heart swelling with love. "And you've given me a reason to believe in everything."

They sat there in silence, wrapped in each other's warmth, as the world seemed to hold its breath, waiting for the moment when their forever would begin.

CHAPTER 22

A Day to Remember

The morning of the wedding dawned bright and crisp, sunlight spilling over the rolling hills of Briarwood Estate. The vineyard buzzed softly with activity—florists arranging simple, elegant bouquets, caterers setting tables draped in white linens beneath the open sky. Sunlight danced across the chairs by the waterfall, arranged perfectly to form an aisle that met the shimmering edge of the lake off to the side of the waterfall.

Eli stood in front of the mirror in the cabin they'd rented for the weekend at the estate which was in a secluded part of the property surrounded by tall pine trees, nervously adjusting his tie. Jenny sat across the room, coffee in hand, watching him with a fond, amused smile.

"Relax," she said, setting her mug down gently. "You look perfect."

Eli turned, his blue eyes wide with worry. "What if I trip? What if I say the wrong thing? What if—"

Jenny held up a hand, cutting him off. "How about you stop overthinking and remember—Matthew loves you, period. Honestly, Eli, you could tumble down the aisle, and he'd still call it the best day of his life."

Eli smiled nervously. "You're right. I just... I want this to be perfect."

Jenny stood and crossed the room to adjust his lapel. "It already is, because it's you two. Now, deep breath."

Eli nodded, inhaling slowly. "Thanks, Jenny."

She paused, her eyes softening. "Eli, I've seen Matthew endure so much. He's been hurt in ways he didn't deserve, and for a long time, I didn't think anyone could make him truly happy. But then you showed up. And I've never seen him like this—so full of life, so... him." Her voice cracked, and she blinked back tears. "Thank you. Thank you for loving him the way he deserves."

Eli's cheeks flushed, his throat tightening with emotion. "I don't know what to say."

Jenny smiled through her tears. "Just keep being you. That's all he needs."

Eli nodded, voice soft and certain. "I will. Always."

Matthew's Morning

Meanwhile, Matthew stood in the vineyard's main tasting room, surrounded by Claire and a few of his groomsmen. He was impeccably dressed in a tailored suit, his usual calm demeanor replaced by a restless energy that hovered somewhere between excitement and nerves.

Claire smirked as she handed him a glass of sparkling wine. "Drink this before you start pacing a hole in the floor."

Matthew chuckled, raising the glass to his lips. "I'm not pacing."

"Not yet," one of his groomsmen teased, drawing a laugh from the group.

The wine in Matthew's glass was a sparkling Riesling from Briarwood Estate—one of the vineyard's most acclaimed offerings. The estate was known for its impeccable wines, crafted from the finest grapes of the Finger Lakes region. Matthew had worked closely with the vineyard's assistant winemakers while their head winemaker Mr. Latham was away to select standout bottles for the celebration—an unoaked stainless-steel Chardonnay and a bold Cabernet from exceptional vintages.

As the laughter quieted, Matthew turned toward the window, gazing out at the endless rows of grapevines, the glimmering lake beyond, and the carefully arranged chairs by the waterfall. A deep sense of peace settled over him.

"It's really happening," he murmured.

Claire stepped beside him, her expression soft and sincere. "It's happening. And it's going to be beautiful—just like you two. Meant to be."

Matthew smiled, the nerves easing as thoughts of Eli filled his heart. "Thank you, Claire. For everything."

She grinned. "That's what best friends are for. Now, let's get you married."

The Ceremony

As guests began to arrive, the vineyard buzzed with a gentle excitement, the calm of earlier preparations giving way to joyous anticipation. The chairs by the waterfall filled steadily, soft murmurs and warm greetings weaving through the air. The cascading sound of the waterfall mingled seamlessly with the delicate strains of a string quartet, their melodies floating lightly on the spring breeze.

Eli stood at the end of the aisle, his heart pounding like a drum. Then, through the soft crowd and swaying vines, he saw Matthew appear, calm, composed, and radiating the quiet confidence that had always grounded him. Their eyes met, and for a heartbeat, the world fell away. Everything else faded into the background, leaving only the steady pulse of love and connection between them.

With each step Eli took down the aisle, he felt the weight of the moment settle deeper into his soul. The nervous fluttering inside transformed into something steadier—an unshakable certainty that this was where he was meant to be. By the time he reached Matthew, the quiet joy between them spoke louder than any words could.

Aunt Margot and Uncle Joe's Moment

Just as the officiant began to speak, a sudden commotion erupted in the second row. Aunt Margot, resplendent in a bright floral dress and an oversized hat, shot a sharp glare at Uncle Joe.

"Did you just take my program?" she snapped, loud enough for the entire ceremony to hear.

Uncle Joe, completely unbothered, waved the program in the air like a flag. "You weren't using it! I needed it to fan myself!"

Margot huffed, snatching it back with a dramatic flair. "You have your own!"

"Mine's under the chair somewhere," Joe grumbled, leaning over to search.

Margot crossed her arms, clearly unimpressed. "Well, if you'd stop losing things, maybe—"

Before she could finish, Joe suddenly tipped too far forward, nearly toppling out of his chair. His legs flailed comically as he tried to regain balance. The crowd gasped, then laughter rippled through the guests as Joe sat upright, brushing himself off and muttering, "I'm fine, I'm fine."

Even the officiant couldn't suppress a chuckle. "Well, it seems love and laughter are already filling the air today."

Matthew leaned close to Eli, whispering, "At least they're reliably chaotic."

Eli chuckled softly, the tension in his chest easing. The moment—unexpected and imperfect—broke the ice for everyone, making the ceremony feel all the more intimate and joyful.

The Vows

When the laughter subsided, the ceremony continued. Matthew and Eli exchanged vows that left few dry eyes in the crowd. Matthew spoke of the first time he saw Eli—how his smile and blue eyes had captivated him instantly.

"You're my tiny opal," Matthew whispered, his voice just above the waterfall's hush.

Eli's eyes glistened as he slipped the ring onto Matthew's finger. "And you're my heart, Matthew. My home."

The Reception

After the ceremony, guests moved to a nearby clearing nestled between the main wine tasting building and the vineyard, where rows of grapevines stretched toward the horizon and overlooked the shimmering lake. Tables were set beneath twinkling string lights, casting a warm glow over the scene. The atmosphere was lively, filled with laughter and the clinking of glasses. Briarwood Estate wines flowed freely—Rieslings with bright citrus notes, Chardonnays with a crisp finish, and rich reds that embodied the region's finest harvests. Matthew had carefully selected each wine to represent the vineyard's best offerings from its most fruitful years.

Jenny and Claire gave a joint toast that left everyone in stitches, recounting years of watching Matthew grow and teasing him for being "predictably perfect," while praising Eli for balancing him out.

Jenny's tone softened as she raised her glass toward Eli. "And to Eli," she said, her voice trembling with emotion, "for reminding Matthew that life isn't just about plans—it's about love. I've seen him go through so much, and I can't tell you how much it means to see him truly happy. Thank you for loving him the way he deserves."

Eli's cheeks flushed as he nodded, the room erupting in applause.

A Moment Alone

As the reception wound down, Matthew and Eli slipped away to the waterfall in the back of the estate, wrapped in a thick blanket against the crisp night air. Eli settled into Matthew's lap, his head resting against his chest.

"This has been the best day of my life," Eli whispered.

Matthew kissed his temple. "Mine too. And it's just the beginning."

They sat in silence, the sound of the waterfall and the cool breeze wrapping around them like a cocoon. Above them, the stars seemed to shine just for them, marking the start of their forever.

CHAPTER 23

A Honeymoon and a Shadow

The wedding had been a dream—an unforgettable celebration of love and community. But as the first rays of sunlight filtered through the curtains of their cabin at Briarwood Estate with the soft scent of smoke from the firepit that was roaring late into the night before, the weight of a new reality began to settle in.

Matthew woke first. He lay still for a moment, quietly watching Eli sleep beside him. Morning light spilled across the room, casting a soft glow on Eli's features—the way his lashes brushed his cheeks, the slight curve of his lips, like he was dreaming something sweet. Gently, Matthew reached out and brushed a strand of hair from Eli's forehead.

"I'm the luckiest man alive," he whispered.

Eli stirred, his blue eyes fluttering open. A slow smile spread across his face as he met Matthew's gaze. "Good morning, husband."

Matthew chuckled and leaned down to kiss his forehead. "Good morning, my tiny opal."

Eli laughed softly, warm and still a little sleepy. "Do you think it'll ever feel normal? Being married to you?"

Matthew grinned. "I hope it never does. I want it to feel extraordinary every day."

Lingering Shadows

After breakfast, they sat on the porch of their cabin, sipping coffee, listening to the birds singing as the vineyard stretched peacefully before them. But beneath the quiet, a subtle tension tugged at the edges of the morning. Eli stared out at the rows of vines, his hands wrapped tightly around his mug, his expression distant.

Matthew studied him for a moment. "What's on your mind?"

Eli hesitated, his fingers tightening. "It's just... I keep thinking about that letter. I thought with everything we've been through, I'd be past it. But it's still there—in the back of my mind."

Matthew's jaw clenched. That letter—unsigned, veiled in menace—had rattled them both. And though Aaron was back in jail for the arson, there had never been proof he'd sent it. The thought that someone else might still be out there hovered like a low, persistent cloud.

Matthew reached over and took Eli's hand. "You're not alone in this. I'll talk to Sheriff Barnes again once we're back in Willow Creek. But for now... this time is ours. You deserve to enjoy it."

Eli nodded slowly, a faint smile pulling at his lips. "You're right. I'm with you—and that's what matters."

Matthew leaned in, his voice low and steady. "And don't forget—I'll always protect you."

A Tour of Briarwood Estate

Later that afternoon, Matthew surprised Eli with a private tour of Briarwood Estate, led by the head winemaker, Mr. Latham. A tall, wiry man with silver hair and a kind smile, Latham greeted them near the main tasting room.

"Matthew Hawthorne," Latham said warmly, shaking his hand. "It's been years, but I remember you well. One of the most promising young talents we ever had. By the way, your wedding was so beautiful. It was so special that you chose to have it here."

Matthew chuckled. "Thank you, I learned from the best, Mr. Latham. Briarwood is one of my most happy places in the world."

Eli looked between them, intrigued. "What was Matthew like back then?"

Latham grinned, gesturing for them to follow him into the vineyard. "Focused, hardworking, always full of questions. He had an eye for detail that even veteran winemakers envy. I'm not surprised he's made something great of his own."

Eli smiled proudly as they walked between rows of sun-drenched vines. Dappled light danced over the ground as Latham spoke about harvest timing, grape selection, and the delicate balance of fermentation.

Inside the aging cellar, the rich scent of oak and fermenting wine filled the air. Latham poured samples of new experimental wines—a sparkling rosé, a bold Cabernet Franc, and a semi-dry Riesling.

Eli swirled his glass, inhaling thoughtfully before tasting. "The Riesling is crisp—lots of citrus and green apple. Good acidity. I'd pair it with grilled fish or something summery."

Latham raised an eyebrow, clearly impressed. "Well, someone's been paying attention."

Eli flushed, glancing at Matthew. "He's been the best teacher."

Matthew slipped an arm around Eli's waist, beaming. "He's a natural."

Latham chuckled. "You've done well, Matthew. And Eli, you've got a real knack. Ever think about working in wine?"

Eli blushed deeper but smiled brightly. "For now, I'm happy learning from him."

A Romantic Evening

As the sun set over Briarwood Estate, casting the sky in soft pinks and golds, Matthew and Eli returned to their cabin. Dinner had already arrived—elegant yet simple, paired with Briarwood's best Cabernet Franc Reserve.

Eli laughed as he recounted a moment from their tour. "Did you see Mr. Latham's face when I said 'acidity'? I swear his eyebrows nearly flew off."

Matthew chuckled, pouring wine into their glasses. "You impressed him. Honestly, you impressed me too. I'm proud of how far you've come."

Eli set his glass aside and stepped closer. "That's because of you. You believed in me—even when I didn't believe in myself."

Matthew cupped his face, thumb brushing gently along his cheek. "Because I see you. The man you are—and the one you're becoming."

Their kiss began softly, tender and lingering, but quickly deepened. Matthew's hands slipped around Eli's waist, pulling him close. Eli's fingers tangled in Matthew's hair, and the space between them vanished, filled only by warmth, breath, and the quiet promise of forever.

The Second Night as Husbands

Later that evening, the bedroom was softly lit by the glow of the fireplace, casting flickering shadows across the walls. Matthew led Eli to the bed, each touch filled with care and intent. The cool night air seeped through cracks in the window, but the warmth between them made it unnoticeable.

Matthew trailed kisses down Eli's neck, his voice a low murmur. "I love you. Every part of you."

Eli's breath hitched, his hands clutching at Matthew's shoulders. "I love you, too. More than I can ever say."

Matthew's lips moved lower, tracing a path across Eli's collarbone. Each kiss sent shivers through Eli's body, his breathing quickening as Matthew's hands explored him, steady and sure. Matthew took his time, savoring every moment, his kisses traveling further across Eli's chest, his toned stomach, and the delicate curve of his hip.

Eli gasped, his fingers threading through Matthew's hair, pulling him closer. "Matthew," he whispered, his voice trembling with anticipation and need.

Matthew paused, looking up at Eli, his gaze filled with love and reverence. "Are you okay?"

Eli nodded, his cheeks flushed, his blue eyes shining with tears of joy. "I've never felt more right about anything."

Matthew smiled, leaning back up to kiss Eli deeply, their bodies pressing together, their hearts pounding in unison. The weight of the world seemed to fall away as they explored each other, their movements slow and deliberate, every touch and kiss carrying the weight of their love.

When they finally came together, it was unlike anything either of them had ever experienced. The physical connection was powerful, but it was the emotional intimacy that overwhelmed them. They moved in perfect harmony, their bodies and souls entwined in a way that felt sacred.

Eli pressed into Matthew, their bodies fitting like pieces of a puzzle. "I never thought I could feel like this," he whispered, his voice filled with awe.

Matthew kissed him again, his lips brushing against Eli's forehead.

"Neither did I. You're everything to me."

As the night stretched on, they held each other close, their breaths mingling in the quiet room. The glow of the fire bathed them in warmth as they whispered words of love and devotion, their bond deepening with every passing moment.

When they finally drifted to sleep, their bodies entwined beneath the thick quilt, it was with the quiet certainty that they had found something rare and beautiful—a love that was both passionate and profound, unshakable in its depth and strength.

A Whisper of Trouble

The next morning, they walked hand in hand through the vineyard, savoring the cool breeze and the scent of fresh earth. Eli leaned into Matthew, his head resting on his shoulder.

"This place feels like a dream," Eli said softly. "I wish we could stay forever."

Matthew kissed the top of his head. "We'll come back. Whenever you want."

The peaceful morning broke with the buzz of Matthew's phone. He frowned as he glanced at the screen—a text from Sheriff Barnes.

Call me when you can. Something came up.

Matthew's stomach tightened, but he forced a smile for Eli. "Just something from town. I'll handle it later."

Eli looked at him with quiet understanding. "If it's about him, I want to know."

Matthew nodded, his grip on Eli's hand tightening. "You will. I promise."

As they continued their walk, the shadow of the text lingered in Matthew's mind. But for now, he focused on the man beside him and the love they had found, choosing, moment by moment, to hold on to their joy.

CHAPTER 24

Shadows Linger

The soft glow of morning sunlight poured through the cabin's windows, casting warm patterns on the wooden floor. Matthew sat at the bed's edge, watching Eli stir under the thick quilt. His husband. The word echoed in his mind, filling him with a quiet sense of wonder and pride.

Eli stretched and turned toward him, his blue eyes opening slowly. A lazy smile spread across his face. "Morning," he murmured.

Matthew leaned down, brushing a kiss across Eli's forehead. "Good morning, my tiny opal."

Eli laughed softly, his cheeks flushing. "Are you ever going to stop calling me that?"

"Never," Matthew replied with a grin. "It suits you too well."

Echoes of Unease

The peaceful moment was interrupted by the faint buzz of Matthew's phone on the nightstand. His brow furrowed as he picked it up and saw Sheriff Barnes's name. Eli sat up, his smile fading as Matthew answered.

"Matthew, sorry to bother you on your honeymoon," Barnes began, his voice steady but with an undertone of urgency.

"What's going on?" Matthew asked, already bracing himself.

Barnes hesitated. "We've had an incident back in Willow Creek. A package was delivered to your wine shop on North Main Street yesterday. It was addressed to you, but your manager opened it, thinking it was inventory. Inside was... a disturbing letter."

Matthew's jaw set, his hand tightening on the bedframe. "What kind of letter?"

"A threatening one," Barnes said bluntly. "Similar to the one Eli received before. Same handwriting. It referenced your wedding and mentioned your 'perfect life.'"

Matthew's stomach twisted. "Do you think it's Aaron?"

"We're not ruling him out," Barnes replied, "but we don't have definitive proof it's him. Whoever sent it seems determined to rattle you. I wanted to warn you before you got back."

Matthew exhaled slowly, glancing at Eli, who was watching him with wide, worried eyes. "Thanks for letting me know, Sheriff. Keep me updated."

After ending the call, Matthew turned to Eli, his expression guarded.

"What did he say?" Eli asked, his voice trembling.

Matthew hesitated, but he knew there was no point in hiding the truth. "A threatening letter was sent to the shop. Barnes thinks it might be connected to the one you received."

Eli's face paled. "Do they know who sent it?"

Matthew shook his head, moving to sit beside him. "Not yet. But they're investigating. We're safe here, Eli. I promise you."

Eli leaned into Matthew's side, his head resting on his shoulder. "I thought it was over," he whispered. "Why can't they just leave us alone?"

Matthew wrapped an arm around him, his grip firm and protective. "Because people like that feed on fear. But we're not going to let them win. We have each other, and that's all that matters."

Seeking Solace

Later that day, Matthew suggested a walk through the vineyard to clear their minds. Eli agreed, though his hands lingered in Matthew's as they strolled along the rows of grapevines. The late-morning sun warmed the earth, and the faint hum of insects filled the air.

"This place is magical," Eli said softly, his gaze sweeping across the landscape. "It feels like nothing bad could ever happen here."

Matthew stopped and turned to face him, smiling. "That's because this is our space. Nothing can touch us here, Eli. Not letters, not threats—nothing."

Eli smiled faintly, his hands covering Matthew's. "You always know how to make me feel safe."

Matthew kissed him gently, their foreheads touching as they stood together in the quiet vineyard. For a moment, the rest of the world fell away, leaving only the love that bound them.

A Mysterious Note

When they returned to the cabin, Matthew noticed something unusual: a folded piece of paper tucked under the edge of the door. His heart sank as he bent to retrieve it, his hand trembling slightly. Eli stood frozen behind him, his breath catching.

Matthew unfolded the paper, his eyes narrowing as he read the message: "It doesn't end here."

Eli took a step back, his face paling. "Is it...?"

Matthew nodded, crumpling the note in his fist. "It's similar to the others. But how did they know where we are?"

Eli's voice wavered. "Do you think they're watching us?"

Matthew placed a steadying hand on Eli's shoulder. "I don't know. But whoever it is, they're not going to get away with this."

Without hesitation, Matthew called Sheriff Barnes, his voice calm but filled with barely restrained anger. He detailed the note and its delivery, sending photos of the message.

"Someone's clearly escalating," Barnes said. "I'll alert the local authorities near Briarwood. We'll get to the bottom of this."

After the call ended, Matthew turned to Eli, who was sitting on the edge of the bed, his hands clenched tightly in his lap.

"I feel like we're being hunted," Eli said, his voice barely above a whisper.

Matthew knelt in front of him, placing his hands over Eli's. "We're not. We're being tested. And we're stronger than this."

Eli met his gaze, his eyes glistening with tears. "How do you stay so calm?"

"Because I have you," Matthew said simply. "You're my focus. My anchor. And I'll never let anyone take that away from me. I will always protect you and keep you safe."

An Evening of Respite

Despite the tension, Matthew insisted they try to salvage the evening. He opened a bottle of Briarwood's signature unoaked chardonnay, setting it on the table with a spread of cheeses, fresh bread, and honey from a local apiary.

Eli took a sip of the wine, the crispness making his mouth water. "This is amazing. It's like drinking happiness."

Matthew laughed, reaching for his glass. "That's exactly what we need right now."

They toasted to each other, their glasses clinking softly. As the evening wore on, the warmth of the wine and their shared laughter began to ease the weight of the day's events.

Later, they returned to the waterfall, wrapped in a thick blanket. Eli sat on Matthew's lap, his head resting against his chest as they watched the stars. The sound of rushing water filled the air, a soothing backdrop to their whispered conversation.

"I don't know how I got so lucky," Eli said, his voice soft. "You're everything I ever dreamed of."

Matthew kissed the top of his head, his voice tender. "And you're everything I never knew I needed."

A Glimpse of Hope

The next morning, Sheriff Barnes called with unexpected news. "We've identified fingerprints on the letter," he said. "And it's not Aaron's."

Matthew's brow furrowed. "Then who is it?"

Barnes hesitated. "We're still investigating, but this might mean the threat is broader than we thought. I'll keep you posted."

Matthew ended the call, his thoughts racing. He turned to Eli, who had been listening intently. "It's not Aaron."

Eli blinked, his confusion evident. "Then... who?"

Matthew wrapped an arm around him, his grip protective. "Whoever it is, we'll face it together. They won't win, Eli. I promise."

CHAPTER 25

Gratitude and Goodbyes

The morning sunlight filtered into the cozy cabin at Briarwood Estate, casting soft patterns on the wooden walls. Matthew stretched as he rose from the bed, glancing back at Eli, who was still tangled in the blankets, his face peaceful in sleep. They had just a few more days at Briarwood before heading home to Willow Creek, and Matthew wanted to make the most of it. But first, there was something they needed to do.

Matthew set the coffee to brew, then began packing a case of wine, choosing each bottle with care from Briarwood's finest: their celebrated Riesling, the crisp stainless-steel–fermented Chardonnay, and a bold Cabernet Franc. He added a rosé — a sentimental favorite from their honeymoon.

"Why are you up so early?" Eli's voice, still thick with sleep, drifted into the quiet. He padded into the kitchen, hair adorably tousled, blue eyes blinking against the morning light.

"Morning, my tiny opal," Matthew said, kissing his forehead with a smile. "I'm putting together a thank-you for the local sheriff's office."

Eli perked up immediately, his legs bouncing slightly as he grinned. "Wine's a good start, but you have to include donuts."

Matthew raised an eyebrow, amused. "Donuts?"

"Absolutely. You can't thank law enforcement without something sweet," Eli insisted, grabbing a notepad to make a list. "We need at least two boxes—maple bacon, chocolate glazed, and jelly-filled."

Matthew chuckled, his chest warming at Eli's enthusiasm. "You and that army of sweet teeth."

Eli corrected him with a playful grin. "Sweet teeth. The whole lot of them."

A Stop at the Local Sheriff's Office

Later that morning, Matthew and Eli arrived at the sheriff's office near Briarwood Estate. Sheriff Latham, a tall man with a weathered face and a no-nonsense demeanor, greeted them at the front desk. His gruff exterior softened when he saw the couple walk in—Matthew holding the wine case and Eli balancing two large boxes of donuts.

"Sheriff Latham," Matthew began, setting the case on the counter, "we wanted to say thank you for everything you've done to keep us safe during our time here."

Eli added, his grin infectious, "And for donuts. Because no one can fight crime without sugar."

Latham chuckled, shaking his head. "You two didn't have to do this, but I'm not about to turn down donuts—or wine."

The deputies in the background perked up at the mention of donuts, one of them practically sprinting to the counter. "Maple bacon?" he asked, lifting the lid to check. "You've got my favorite!"

Eli beamed, nudging Matthew. "Told you."

As they chatted briefly with the sheriff and his team, Matthew felt a sense of closure. That chapter—the threats, fear, and sleepless nights—was finally closed. And now, he and Eli could look forward.

Homeward Bound

The drive back to Willow Creek was filled with easy conversation and laughter. Eli's energy was as bright and uncontainable as the midday sun. "Do you think the deputies at home will like jelly-filled donuts as much as Sheriff Latham's team?"

Matthew smirked, his hands steady on the wheel. "I think they'll like anything with sugar, considering how fast those donuts disappeared back there."

Eli leaned back in his seat, watching the trees blur past. "I hope Sheriff Barnes likes his wine. Did you pack enough?"

Matthew shot him an amused glance. "It's a case of six bottles, Eli. That's plenty."

When they arrived in Willow Creek, their first stop was the town's sheriff's office. Sheriff Barnes greeted them with a firm handshake, his usual serious demeanor softening at the sight of Eli holding yet another two boxes of donuts.

"You're spoiling us," Barnes said, his tone dry but appreciative. "First wine, now donuts. What's next?"

Eli grinned. "Maybe cookies next time. But for now, we just wanted to say thanks for everything."

Barnes nodded, his gaze settling on Matthew. "You two didn't have to do this. It's our job to keep people safe, but it means a lot."

Matthew shook his hand again, his voice steady. "You did more than your job. You gave us peace of mind, and we'll never forget that."

The Calm After the Storm

That evening, back in the comfort of their home, Eli flopped onto the couch with a dramatic sigh. "I feel like we've been on a donut delivery tour."

Matthew laughed, sitting beside him and pulling him close. "You loved every second of it."

Eli rested his head on Matthew's shoulder, his voice soft. "I did. But I love being here with you even more."

They sat in comfortable silence for a while, the house settling around them. The heavy weight of the past few months slowly lifted, replaced by the quiet joy of simply being together.

Dreams of Adventure

As the evening stretched on, Matthew glanced at Eli, his expression thoughtful. "You know, now that everything's settled... maybe it's time we start planning that trip."

Eli turned to him, his blue eyes wide with excitement. "You mean the wine tour?"

Matthew nodded. "Two weeks. Tuscany ... all the places I've always wanted to show you."

Eli's legs bounced excitedly, his grin spreading across his face. "You mean it? We're really doing this?"

Matthew chuckled, brushing a strand of hair from Eli's forehead. "I mean it. It's time for an adventure."

Eli wrapped his arms around Matthew, his voice muffled against his chest. "I've never been more excited for anything in my life."

Matthew held him close, his heart full. "Then let's make it the trip of our lives."

CHAPTER 26

A New Horizon

The first rays of morning sunlight crept into the bedroom, bathing the space in a warm, golden glow. Matthew stirred first, his gaze drifting to Eli, who was curled up beside him, his face relaxed in peaceful sleep. It had been nearly a week since they returned from their honeymoon, and life in Willow Creek had settled into a comfortable rhythm. But this morning, a sense of anticipation buzzed in the air.

Matthew slid out of bed carefully, not wanting to disturb Eli, and headed to the kitchen. As the coffee brewed, he pulled out his laptop and began reviewing their plans for the day. They were finally moving forward with their dream, preparing for the two-week international trip they had planned during their honeymoon.

Eli shuffled into the kitchen, hair a charming mess, blue eyes still clouded with sleep. "Good morning," he mumbled, leaning against Matthew for warmth.

Matthew kissed his forehead, his voice soft. "Good morning, my tiny opal. Ready for a day of planning?"

Eli's face lit up, his legs bouncing slightly with excitement as he pulled up a chair at the table. "Are you kidding? I've been thinking about this trip non-stop. I even dreamed about it last night."

Matthew chuckled, setting a steaming mug of coffee in front of him. "Let me guess—you were on a plane, scarfing down donuts."

Eli grinned sheepishly. "Close. I was on a plane, but they gave me cookies. It was magical."

Planning Their Next Adventure

As they went over the itinerary, Matthew's attention to detail shone through. He had planned visits to some of Italy's most iconic wine regions. Each destination promised not only wine education for Eli but also opportunities to immerse themselves in the culture and beauty of the regions.

Eli, on the other hand, was more concerned about the little things. "Do you think I'll get jet lag? What if I don't like the plane food? And what if I forget how to say something in Italian?"

Matthew reached across the table, squeezing Eli's hand. "You'll be fine. We'll tackle it all together. Besides, I'll be there to remind you how to say 'wine' in Italian."

Eli laughed, his nervous energy easing. "Vino, right?"

Matthew smiled. "Exactly. See? You're already ahead of the game."

A Visit to Briarwood Estate

Before their trip, Matthew wanted to stop by Briarwood Estate to finalize some business matters and share their plans with Mr. Latham, the head winemaker who had become a trusted friend. The vineyard was buzzing with activity as they arrived, the workers preparing for the upcoming harvest.

Latham greeted them warmly, his weathered face breaking into a smile. "Matthew! Eli! What brings you back so soon?"

"We wanted to share some news," Matthew said, his excitement evident. "We're leaving for a two-week trip to explore some of the best wine regions in Itlay."

Latham raised an impressed eyebrow. "Now that's a honeymoon follow-up if I've ever heard one. Where are you headed?"

Matthew rattled off the list of destinations, and Latham nodded approvingly. "You're going to love Tuscany. The reds there are unlike anything you've had."

Eli listened intently, his curiosity shining through. "Do they really taste different because of the soil?"

Latham chuckled. "Exactly. Terroir—how the soil, climate, and environment affect the grapes—plays a huge role. Looks like Matthew's been teaching you right."

Eli blushed under the praise, but his smile was wide. "He's the best teacher."

A Bit of Humor

That evening, as they packed for the trip, Eli's endless questions kept Matthew laughing.

"Do you think I'll fit well in the plane seat?" Eli asked, his legs bouncing as he sat cross-legged on the bed.

Matthew turned from the suitcase he was organizing, smirking. "You're tiny, Eli. You'll have legroom for days."

Eli scrunched his face playfully. "Okay, but what about customs? What if I accidentally bring something illegal?"

Matthew laughed, pulling him into a hug. "Then I'll charm our way out of it."

Eli tilted his head, grinning. "You'd use that smile of yours, wouldn't you?"

Matthew leaned down, his voice teasing. "It works on you, doesn't it?"

Eli blushed, swatting his arm. "Stop distracting me. I need to figure out how many pairs of socks to bring."

A Farewell to Willow Creek

The morning of their departure arrived, and they stood outside their house with their suitcases. Jenny and Claire had come to see them off, their usual banter filling the air.

"Don't forget to send pictures," Claire said, hugging Matthew tightly. "And bring me back something fancy from Italy!"

Jenny grinned, pulling Eli into a hug. "Keep Matthew from getting too serious. He needs you to trip him up—literally and lovingly."

Eli laughed, his cheeks flushing. "I'll do my best."

As they climbed into the car, Matthew glanced back at their friends and the town that had become their sanctuary. "We'll be back before you know it."

Claire waved dramatically. "Don't rush! Willow Creek will survive without you—barely."

Taking Off

At the airport, Eli's excitement was palpable. He clutched Matthew's hand as they boarded the plane, his eyes wide as he took in the rows of seats and bustling passengers.

"This is amazing," Eli whispered as they settled into their seats. "I've never seen anything like this."

Matthew smiled, his heart swelling at Eli's childlike wonder. "Wait until we're in the air."

When the plane began to taxi, Eli's grip on Matthew's hand tightened. As the plane lifted off, his eyes widened, and he gasped. "Matthew—we're flying! We're really in the air!"

Matthew chuckled, leaning in. "You're impossible not to love, you know that?"

Eli blushed, his smile radiant. "I can't believe we're doing this."

Looking Ahead

As the plane soared above the clouds, Matthew and Eli leaned their heads together, gazing out the window at the endless expanse of blue sky. Their journey was just beginning, but already, it felt like the start of something extraordinary.

Matthew turned to Eli, his voice soft. "Are you ready for this adventure?"

Eli nodded, his blue eyes shining with excitement. "With you? Always."

CHAPTER 27

High Altitudes and Heartfelt Moments

The plane cruised at 30,000 feet, a sea of clouds rolling beneath them like waves. Eli couldn't tear his gaze away from the window, his awe palpable. Every so often, he would point at something—a glint of sunlight on the horizon, the faint outline of another plane in the distance— and Matthew would glance over with a soft smile.

"You're going to use up all your excitement before we even land," Matthew teased, leaning back in his seat.

Eli turned to him, his blue eyes alight with wonder. "There's no way. I've never even imagined the world could look like this."

Matthew's heart swelled as he reached for Eli's hand. "Just wait. The best part hasn't even started."

A Mid-Air Surprise

As the flight attendants rolled their carts down the aisles, Eli's eyes lit up. "Is it snack time?" he asked, his legs bouncing with excitement.

Matthew chuckled. "It's snack time."

When the attendant reached their row, Eli leaned forward eagerly. "Do you have cookies?"

The attendant handed him a small package of shortbread cookies, and Eli's face lit up like he'd just won the lottery. "This is amazing," he declared, tearing into the package.

A moment later, he frowned, holding up one of the cookies. "Matthew, why is this cookie shaped like a plane? Is that… normal?"

Matthew bit his lip, struggling to hold back laughter. "Yes, Eli. It's just a fun touch for the flight."

Eli popped the cookie into his mouth, chewing thoughtfully. "It's good. But now I feel weird eating a plane while we're flying."

That was it. Matthew burst into laughter, clutching his stomach as tears sprang to his eyes. "Only you would think of that," he managed between breaths.

Eli huffed, cheeks flushing pink. "You're terrible."

"And you're adorable," Matthew said, wiping his eyes. "Please never change."

A Moment of Hilarity

About halfway through the flight, Eli decided to explore the in-flight entertainment system. After a few minutes of fiddling with the touchscreen, he managed to start a movie—only the volume blasted through the headphones, making him jump in his seat.

Matthew, startled, turned to see Eli fumbling with the controls, his face bright red. "What happened?" he asked, barely containing his laughter.

"I think I broke it!" Eli whispered frantically, yanking the headphones off his head.

Matthew leaned over, taking the screen controls from Eli's trembling hands. "You didn't break it. You just turned the volume all the way up."

Eli groaned, burying his face in his hands. "I'm so bad at this."

Matthew burst into laughter, his shoulders shaking as he adjusted the settings. "You're not bad at it. You're just... enthusiastic."

Eli peeked through his fingers, cheeks still flushed. "Don't laugh at me."

"I'm not laughing at you," Matthew said, eyes watering. "I'm laughing because you're hilarious. There's a difference."

Eli huffed but couldn't hide the small smile tugging at his lips. "You're lucky I love you."

Matthew kissed the top of his head, his laughter finally subsiding. "And I'm lucky you do."

The Landing

The descent into Florence brought a fresh wave of excitement. Eli's grip on Matthew's hand tightened as the plane tilted, revealing a breathtaking view of the rolling Tuscan hills below. The landscape stretched out like a living tapestry — vineyards, olive groves, and terra-cotta rooftops bathed in the soft glow of late afternoon sun.

"This is it," Matthew whispered. "Tuscany."

Eli remained silent, eyes fixed on the beauty beneath them. When the plane finally touched down, he let out a breath he hadn't realized he'd been holding. "That was... incredible."

Matthew squeezed his hand gently. "And this is only the beginning."

A Sentimental Return

The next morning, Matthew drove them along a winding gravel road that cut through fields of grapevines, their leaves still shimmering with morning dew. In the distance, a rustic stone building stood proudly among tall cypress trees, the heart of the vineyard nestled in the Tuscan countryside.

"This vineyard," Matthew said reverently, "was my first international wine experience. I was in my twenties, scraping together just enough money to make the trip. But being here... it changed everything."

Eli glanced at him, his eyes soft with affection. "And now you're back. With me."

Matthew smiled, their fingers brushing as they walked toward the main building. "It feels right."

They were greeted warmly by Matteo, the vineyard's owner, who remembered Matthew from years ago. "Ah, the young sommelier returns! And with someone special this time."

Matthew introduced Eli, who blushed slightly under Matteo's kind gaze. "He's my heart," Matthew said without hesitation.

Matteo led them through the vineyard, sharing stories about the unique terroir and its influence on the wines. Eli listened intently, asking thoughtful questions about the soil, the climate, and the aging process—each one showing just how much he'd learned from Matthew.

"You've taught him well," Matteo said, nodding appreciatively at Matthew.

Matthew's chest swelled with pride. "He's a natural."

A Romantic Tasting

The tour ended on a secluded terrace overlooking the vineyard, where a table was elegantly set with fine glassware and plates of fresh bread, local cheeses, and olives. Matteo poured their first glass, a rich Brunello, and began to share their storied history.

Eli swirled the wine in his glass, carefully mimicking Matthew's technique. When he took a sip, his eyes widened in surprise. "It's... like it has layers. I can taste the fruit, but there's something deeper beneath."

Matteo's face lit up with a proud smile. "Perfectly said! You have a gift."

Eli blushed, glancing shyly at Matthew. "Matthew's the best teacher I could ask for."

As the sun dipped below the horizon, painting the sky in breathtaking shades of gold and pink, Matthew and Eli settled into a quiet, shared contentment. Matthew reached for Eli's hand, his thumb tracing soft, comforting circles along his skin.

"Thank you for bringing me here," Eli whispered, his voice thick with emotion.

Matthew leaned in, pressing a tender kiss to Eli's temple. "Thank you for letting me share it with you."

Back at the Villa

That evening, they returned to their villa, their hearts full from the day's experiences. Matthew lit a fire in the stone hearth while Eli prepared a small platter of fruit and cheese. They opened another bottle of wine they had purchased at the vineyard, savoring its rich aroma.

As they settled on the plush rug in front of the fire, Eli rested his head against Matthew's chest. "This is the best day I've ever had," he murmured, his voice barely above a whisper.

Matthew kissed the top of his head, his own voice thick with emotion. "And this is just the start, my tiny opal."

Eli tilted his head to look up at him, his blue eyes shimmering in the flickering firelight. "I love you."

Matthew smiled, his hand gently cupping Eli's cheek. "I love you, too. Always."

CHAPTER 28

A Tuscan Dream

The Tuscan sun stretched across the horizon, casting a golden glow over the countryside as Matthew and Eli awoke in their villa. The crisp morning air carried the faint scent of lavender and freshly turned soil. Eli stirred first, his legs stretching under the covers as he let out a small, contented sigh. He turned to Matthew, who was already watching him with a soft smile.

"Morning, my tiny opal," Matthew said warmly, brushing Eli's cheek and hair with soft affection. Eli blushed, the nickname still making his heart flutter.

"Good morning. What's on the agenda today?" Eli asked, eyes bright with curiosity.

Matthew propped himself up on one elbow, his hand resting lightly on Eli's jaw as he admired him. "We're heading to a vineyard I've always admired. They have a reputation for bold reds and stunning views, and I've arranged for us to have a private blending session with the winemaker."

Eli's eyes widened, his legs bouncing slightly under the sheets. "A blending session? Wait—like we're actually making our own wine?"

Matthew chuckled. "Exactly. You'll get to create something unique, something that's entirely yours."

Eli beamed, his excitement palpable. "I can't wait. But first—breakfast."

Matthew paused, tilting his head thoughtfully. "But before we dive into all that, is there anything you'd like to do today? Something that's been on your mind?"

Eli shook his head, his expression softening. "I love everything you plan. You've been to these places before, and you know them so well. I trust you to show me all the best parts. Honestly, I just like watching you light up when you talk about these things."

Matthew smiled, leaning down to kiss his forehead. "You're incredible, you know that?"

Eli laughed softly, shrugging. "I just know I'm lucky."

A Sweet Start

The villa's dining room was a cozy haven of rustic charm, with wooden beams overhead and a roaring fire in the hearth. The table was set with a spread of fresh pastries, fruit, and honey from the local apiary. Eli's eyes locked onto a tray of sugar-dusted croissants.

"These look amazing," he said, grabbing one and taking a bite. His eyes lit up. "It's like eating a cloud."

Matthew laughed softly, pouring them both glasses of freshly squeezed orange juice. "You and your sweet teeth."

Eli grinned, his legs swinging under the table. "Can you blame me? Italy makes everything taste better."

Matthew took a bite of his own croissant, nodding. "You're not wrong. This honey? Unreal."

As they lingered over breakfast, Matthew went over the day's plans in detail. "After the vineyard, I thought we'd take a walk through the nearby olive groves. The olive groves are supposed to glow at sunset."

Eli leaned forward, his face eager. "And then?"

Matthew smirked. "Then... you'll just have to wait and see."

Eli rested his chin in his hand, watching Matthew fondly. "I'm happy just following your lead. You've been to these places before, and everything you pick always turns out perfect."

Matthew reached across the table, taking Eli's hand. "Then let's make today unforgettable."

A Vineyard Adventure

The drive to the vineyard was a scenic journey through winding roads flanked by cypress trees and golden fields. When they arrived, Eli's jaw dropped. The vineyard sprawled across the hillside, its vines stretching toward the horizon. A grand stone building sat at the center, its ivy-covered walls glistening in the morning sun.

"This place is... unreal," Eli breathed as he stepped out.

Matthew placed a hand on his lower back, guiding him toward the entrance. "Just wait until you meet the winemaker. He's a legend in this region."

Inside, they were greeted by Luca, a jovial man with silver-streaked hair and a warm smile. "Matthew! It's been years," Luca said, pulling him into a friendly embrace. His gaze shifted to Eli. "And who is this?"

Matthew smiled, his hand resting on Eli's shoulder. "This is my husband, Eli."

Eli blushed under Luca's kind gaze. "It's nice to meet you."

"The pleasure is mine," Luca replied. "Come, let's get started."

Creating a Blend

Luca led them to a sunlit room filled with barrels, bottles, and glass pipettes. He explained the process of blending, showing them how to measure and mix different wines to create a harmonious balance of flavors.

Eli listened intently, his curiosity evident. When it was his turn to create a blend, he approached the task with careful precision, taking small sips and making notes on a clipboard.

"This one," Eli said, holding up a glass, "has a nice fruitiness, but it needs more body. Maybe a splash of the Merlot?"

Luca raised an impressed eyebrow. "You have a good instinct."

Matthew watched with pride as Eli adjusted his blend, his small frame dwarfed by the towering barrels around him. When Eli finally presented his finished wine, Luca took a sip and nodded approvingly.

"Perfectly balanced," Luca declared. "You've created something truly special."

Eli turned to Matthew, his face glowing. "What do you think?"

Matthew took a sip, savoring the complex layers of flavor. "It's incredible. Just like you."

Eli blushed, his smile radiant. "I couldn't have done it without you."

A Sunset Stroll

As the day transitioned into evening, Matthew and Eli wandered through the olive groves near the vineyard. The setting sun painted the landscape in hues of gold and amber, casting long shadows across the rolling hills.

Eli slipped his hand into Matthew's, his grip firm yet gentle. "This is perfect," he said softly. "I feel like I'm walking through a dream."

Matthew stopped, pulling Eli closer. "You are my dream, Eli. Everything about this trip—everything about us—it's exactly what I've always hoped for in life."

Eli rested his head against Matthew's chest, his voice a whisper. "I love you."

Matthew tilted his chin up, pressing a tender kiss to his lips. "And I love you. Forever and always."

A Cozy Evening

Back at the villa, the fireplace crackled as they curled up on the couch with glasses of wine. Eli leaned against Matthew, his legs tucked under him, as they recounted the day's adventures.

"Will we ever come back here?" Eli asked, his voice drowsy.

Matthew kissed the top of his head. "Absolutely. This is just the beginning, Eli. We have so many more places to explore."

Eli smiled, his eyes drifting closed. "As long as I'm with you, anywhere will feel like home."

Matthew held him close, his heart full. As the flames danced in the fireplace, he realized that this trip wasn't just about wine or adventure—it was about building a life together, one unforgettable moment at a time.

CHAPTER 29

Uncorking the Unexpected

The villa's shutters creaked gently in the morning breeze as the first light of dawn painted the hills in soft golds and pinks. Eli stretched lazily under the crisp linen sheets, his short hair mussed from sleep. Matthew was already up, standing by the window with a steaming cup of coffee in hand, gazing out at the endless rows of vines stretching into the horizon.

"Good morning," Eli mumbled, rubbing his eyes and pushing himself upright.

Matthew turned, his lips curling into a soft smile. "Morning, sleepyhead. Ready for another day in paradise?"

Eli propped himself up on his elbows, his expression dreamy. "Do you think it's possible to get used to this? Waking up in Tuscany, drinking coffee with you, and having nothing but vineyards around us?"

Matthew chuckled, setting his mug down on the bedside table. He leaned down, brushing a hand over Eli's hair before letting his thumb trace along his cheek. "It's dangerous. We might never leave."

Eli grinned, leaning into Matthew's touch. "I wouldn't mind."

Matthew's phone buzzed softly on the nightstand, breaking the quiet moment. He glanced at the screen and frowned slightly. "Looks like we have a surprise visitor today."

Eli raised an eyebrow, curiosity piqued. "A surprise? Here?"

Matthew nodded, standing to grab his jacket. "Luca mentioned an old friend from the wine community is in town. He wants to meet us—and maybe share something special."

Eli's eyes sparkled with anticipation. "Now I'm even more excited. Tuscany just keeps getting better."

They shared a smile, ready to uncork whatever unexpected moments the day would bring.

A Change of Plans

After a leisurely breakfast on the villa's terrace, Matthew unfolded their itinerary for the day. "We were supposed to visit another vineyard this morning," he said, scanning the list, "but I just got an email saying their tasting room is closed today. Something about unexpected renovations."

Eli tilted his head, his legs swinging under the table. "What should we do instead?"

Matthew smirked, setting the paper down. "That's the beauty of being on vacation—we can do whatever we want. Any ideas?"

Eli thought for a moment, his eyes scanning the hills beyond the villa. "What if we explore one of the smaller villages nearby? You said they have markets, right?"

Matthew nodded, intrigued. "They do. Let's find one. A quiet day wandering sounds perfect."

He folded up the itinerary, standing to gather their things. As he did, a thought seemed to cross his mind.

"Eli?"

"Yeah?" Eli replied, looking up from his half-finished pastry.

Matthew's tone softened. "Have you ever thought about having kids?"

Eli blinked, his eyes opening wide, surprised by the question but not uncomfortable. A small smile spread across his face as he leaned back in his chair, his legs starting to bounce. "I've thought about it," he admitted. "I think I'd love that—starting a little family with you."

Matthew's heart swelled at Eli's honesty, but he kept his tone light, nodding thoughtfully. "Me too. Just something to think about for the future."

Eli reached across the table, placing his hand over Matthew's. "I'd like that. A lot."

Matthew squeezed his hand gently. "We'll talk more about it when the time's right."

Eli nodded, his face glowing with a quiet joy. "Okay."

The Village Market

The drive to the village was short but scenic, the winding roads lined with olive groves and the occasional rustic farmhouse. The market was nestled in the heart of the village, a bustling square filled with colorful stalls offering everything from handmade pottery to freshly baked bread.

Eli wandered from booth to booth, his excitement contagious. He picked up jars of local honey, sampled cured meats, and admired delicate glass ornaments that sparkled in the sunlight. Every so often, he would glance back at Matthew, holding up his latest discovery like a child showing off a treasure.

At one booth, an older woman smiled warmly as Eli admired her handmade scarves. "For your wife?" she asked in heavily accented English.

Eli blushed, shaking his head. "For my husband."

The woman's eyes lit up with understanding. "Ah, amore. Then he is very lucky."

Eli glanced over at Matthew, who was inspecting a selection of balsamic glazes nearby, and smiled. "I'm the lucky one."

A Suspenseful Turn

The sunlit market buzzed with life—children laughing, merchants calling out their wares, and the scent of ripe tomatoes and fresh bread filling the air. Matthew had just begun to relax, enjoying the simple pleasure of Eli's hand in his, when a shift in the atmosphere tugged at his senses.

It was subtle at first—a flicker of movement, a glance held too long. Matthew's instincts kicked in. He had spent too many years in places where danger came disguised in smiles and stillness. His gaze locked onto a man standing near a fruit stall, seemingly casual, yet too aware.

At first, Matthew tried to shake it off. Maybe the man was just people-watching, enjoying the bustle like any other tourist. But as they moved from one stall to another, Matthew kept spotting him—always nearby, always pretending to look elsewhere. The way the man adjusted his position to stay within earshot seemed like no coincidence.

Matthew's grip on Eli's hand tightened slightly.

Eli gave a small smile, though his eyes held a flicker of unease. "I see the guy following us. Promise you won't let anything happen to us?"

Matthew's voice was calm, but edged with resolve. "Always. No matter what."

He squeezed Eli's hand, their silent reassurance weaving a protective shield around them. Outside, the village life carried on—blissfully unaware of the shadow threading its way through their perfect Tuscan day.

But then, just as Matthew was about to confront the man, the "threat" revealed itself. The stranger stepped forward with an awkward wave, holding out a pair of sunglasses.

"Scusate! You dropped these back at the olive oil stand!" he said, slightly out of breath. "I tried to catch up, but you walk like... very fast Americans!"

Matthew blinked. Eli stifled a laugh. The man grinned, gave them the sunglasses, and wandered off to buy grapes—leaving Matthew and Eli with nothing more dangerous than a mildly bruised ego and a new inside joke about "the deadly sunglass stalker of Tuscany."

A Return to Calm

As the day went on, the unsettling moment at the market faded into the background. They returned to their villa with a basket full of local treats and spent the afternoon preparing a simple meal together. Eli insisted on making dessert—a tiramisu he'd learned to make from a YouTube video before their trip.

"It's not authentic," he said as he layered mascarpone over espresso-soaked ladyfingers, "but it's delicious."

Matthew watched him work, his heart swelling with affection. "You could make a bowl of cereal, and I'd still think it's the best meal ever."

Eli laughed, his legs bouncing with delight. "You're completely biased."

"Maybe," Matthew admitted, leaning in to steal a quick kiss. "But I'm also right."

An Evening Revelation

The soft clink of their glasses echoed gently in the warm night air as a breeze carried the scent of lavender from the nearby garden. The world felt still and sacred in that moment, as if time had paused just for them.

Matthew's hand lingered on Eli's knee, the simple touch grounding them both in a shared promise. "No matter what comes, we face it together," he whispered, his eyes reflecting the shimmer of stars above.

Eli nodded, feeling the strength of that vow wrap around him like a shield. "Together," he echoed, his voice steady and sure.

They leaned into each other, the quiet peace of the Tuscan night cradling their hearts — a perfect end to a day marked by beauty, vulnerability, and unshakable love.

Looking Ahead

That night, under a blanket of stars, their whispered plans wove dreams of laughter, shared meals, and sparkling toasts. The road ahead shimmered with possibility, each new experience a thread in the tapestry they were creating together.

Matthew folded the map carefully, his fingers brushing Eli's hand once more. "No matter where this takes us, we'll make it unforgettable."

Eli smiled, his heart full. "With you, every moment already is."

And as the Tuscan night embraced them, love remained their constant compass—steady, true, and glowing brighter than ever.

CHAPTER 30

A Sparkling Adventure

Matthew grabbed the keys from the table and led Eli down the stone steps to the car waiting in the courtyard. The drive to the vineyard was a breeze, winding through sun-dappled roads framed by cypress trees and golden fields.

When they arrived, the sparkling vineyard glittered in the sunlight, the vines heavy with clusters of grapes ready for harvest. Luca, their host from before, greeted them with a broad grin. "Welcome back, my friends! Ready to see how magic is made?"

Matthew winked at Eli. "Ready as ever."

Inside the cool, vaulted tasting room, Luca explained the meticulous process of crafting sparkling wines — the delicate balance of timing, temperature, and patience. Eli listened intently, eyes wide with fascination.

Then came the moment they'd been waiting for: the private tasting. Glasses clinked, bubbles danced on their tongues, and Eli's face lit up with every sip. "This is like liquid joy," he breathed.

Matthew smiled, watching Eli's delight. "Told you you'd love it."

After the tasting, they strolled through the sunlit vineyards, their hands intertwined. Matthew's surprise awaited at the end of the path: a quaint picnic setup beneath a canopy of olive branches, complete with fresh bread, local cheeses, and a bottle of their favorite sparkling wine.

Eli's eyes shimmered. "You really do know how to make every moment special."

Matthew pulled him close, whispering, "Only because you make every moment worth it."

As the sun dipped low, casting the vineyard in a golden glow, they toasted to love, laughter, and a sparkling adventure they'd never forget.

A Vineyard with a View

The drive to the vineyard was nothing short of breathtaking. Winding roads led them past golden fields, sun-drenched olive groves, and sleepy villages that seemed untouched by time. Each told you revealed a postcard-perfect landscape, and Eli could barely contain his excitement as he watched the world unfold outside the car window.

When they finally arrived, Eli's jaw nearly dropped.

Perched atop a hill, the vineyard overlooked a sweeping valley of grapevines stretching as far as the eye could see. The estate itself was a grand stone villa with ivy creeping up its ancient walls, the kind of place that seemed to exist only in paintings and dreams. The real difference- this estate had two helipads. Just beyond it, an outdoor terrace offered a panoramic view of the countryside, where rows of neatly cultivated vines stretched toward the horizon.

"This looks like something out of a dream," Eli murmured as he stepped out of the car, his eyes scanning every inch of the breathtaking scenery.

Matthew smiled, watching the way Eli's gaze drank it all in, the way he looked so effortlessly captivated by the world around him. "Wait until you taste the wine."

Before Eli could respond, a distinguished-looking man in his sixties approached, dressed in a tailored vest and a crisp white shirt. His gray hair was neatly combed back, and there was a warmth in his deep-set eyes that made him instantly welcoming.

"Ah, Matthew! It's been too long," he said warmly, shaking Matthew's hand.

"Stefano," Matthew greeted, his voice filled with genuine warmth. "It's good to be back."

Stefano turned to Eli, his keen eyes taking him in with a knowing smile. "And this must be the lucky man who stole your heart."

Eli's cheeks immediately turned pink as he extended a hand. "It's nice to meet you."

Stefano shook his hand firmly, then gestured toward the terrace. "Come. Let's begin."

A Taste of the Best

Matthew's eyes softened as he watched Eli soak in every moment. "You're catching on faster than I expected. Soon, you'll be teaching me a thing or two."

Eli laughed, the sound light and full of joy. "Maybe. But for now, I'm happy learning from you."

Stefano joined in the laughter, raising his glass in a toast. "To new friendships, fine wine, and the magic of Tuscany."

They clinked glasses, the sparkling wine shimmering between them like liquid sunlight. As the bubbles danced on their tongues, so did the sense of connection to the land, to the craft, and to each other.

The afternoon stretched on, filled with stories, laughter, and the gentle Tuscan breeze. It was a moment perfectly uncorked, one they would savor long after the last drop.

A Surprise Adventure

After the tasting, Matthew took Eli's hand with a mischievous smile. "Ready for your surprise?"

Eli's eyes sparkled with curiosity. "More than ready."

They drove for about an hour, the landscape shifting from vineyard-covered hills to rugged cliffs overlooking the Tyrrhenian Sea. When Matthew pulled into a small coastal village, Eli's breath caught.

"The ocean!" he exclaimed, practically bouncing with excitement.

Matthew grinned, loving the way Eli's face lit up. "I thought you'd like to see another side of Tuscany."

Eli didn't hesitate. "Let's go down to the beach!"

Matthew pulled a small bag from the back seat. "Already packed towels and everything."

The beach was a hidden gem—golden sands stretched beneath the warm sun, meeting waters so turquoise they seemed unreal. The waves lapped gently at the shore, and the salty breeze tousled Eli's hair. He kicked off his shoes immediately, wiggling his toes in the soft sand.

Matthew watched him with affection. "You look like a kid discovering summer for the first time."

Eli giggled, spinning around. "I feel like one."

They spent the afternoon like children, splashing and chasing each other in the shallow waves. Matthew, usually composed and refined, laughed freely, swept up by Eli's infectious joy. When Eli spotted a tiny crab skittering across the sand, he tried to chase it—only to yelp when it turned, pincers raised.

Matthew doubled over with laughter. "It's like your own tiny bodyguard."

Eli pouted. "I don't trust it."

Matthew pulled him into a warm embrace. "You don't have to. You've got me."

Eli smiled softly, pressing a damp kiss to Matthew's shoulder. "I wouldn't want anyone else."

As the sky shifted from purple to deep orange, Matthew reached into the bag and pulled out the sparkling wine they'd bought earlier. With practiced ease, he popped the cork and poured two glasses.

"To more days like this," Matthew said, raising his glass.

"To us," Eli replied, clinking his glass gently against Matthew's.

They sipped their wine as the stars began to twinkle overhead and the waves whispered their ancient secrets. In that perfect moment, the world felt still, and theirs alone.

CHAPTER 31

The Unexpected Storm

Morning light filtered softly through the villa's shutters, casting warm golden stripes across the bedroom floor. Eli stirred beneath the crisp linen sheets, stretching slowly before rolling toward Matthew. He found him already awake, propped on one elbow, watching him with that familiar, lazy smile that always made his heart skip.

"Morning, my tiny opal," Matthew murmured, his fingertips brushing lightly along Eli's jaw before tracing the delicate curve of his cheek.

Eli blinked up at him, caught somewhere between sleep and wakefulness. "Morning." A yawn escaped before a small, sleepy smile tugged at his lips. "I think I'm really getting used to waking up in paradise."

Matthew chuckled softly, pressing a lingering kiss to Eli's temple. "That's dangerous. I might have to find a way to keep you here forever."

Eli stretched again, legs kicking lightly under the sheets, a dreamy sigh escaping him. "Could be worse."

Matthew pushed himself up to sit at the edge of the bed, his gaze turning thoughtful. "We should get an early start today. The mountains are beautiful this time of day. There's a little village along the way where we can stop for breakfast."

Eli smiled, sitting up and swinging his legs off the bed. "That sounds perfect."

Outside, the sky held a rare stillness—clear, but with an almost imperceptible weight in the air, as if the landscape was holding its breath. Neither of them noticed yet, but the calm would soon give way to something unexpected.

A Road Through the Clouds

The drive took them up into the Tuscan hills, winding through narrow roads that overlooked breathtaking valleys below. Tall cypress trees stood like guardians, flanking roads that wound through vineyards and weathered stone cottages.

They had packed up everything before leaving the villa originally planning just a scenic drive before checking into a new hotel later that evening. What was meant to be a lazy daytrip had quickly shifted into a full departure, their suitcases now tucked in the trunk, just in case.

Eli's face was practically pressed to the window, breath fogging the glass as he pointed out small farms, ancient churches tucked into the hillsides, and clusters of olive trees.

"This is like something out of a painting," he murmured, eyes wide with awe. "I know I keep saying it, but it really is."

Matthew glanced over with a soft smile. "That's why I love it here. There's a stillness to the place. Like time moves slower, and everyone just... breathes."

Eli turned to watch Matthew's hands steady on the steering wheel, the calm confidence he wore so naturally here. "You could live here, couldn't you?"

Matthew smirked. "Couldn't you?"

Eli nodded slowly. "Only if you were with me."

Matthew reached over, squeezing his knee gently. "Good answer."

But as they crested the next hill, the perfect blue sky began to shift. Thick clouds rolled in swiftly, swallowing the sunlight and casting a sudden gray veil over the landscape. The wind picked up, whipping through the cypress and rattling the car with sharp gusts.

Matthew frowned, eyes flicking to the horizon. "That's odd. The forecast didn't call for rain today."

Eli's gaze followed the darkening sky, his excitement giving way to unease. "That doesn't look like normal rain clouds."

And he was right. Within moments, the wind escalated into fierce gusts that rattled the windows and sent leaves and dust swirling through the air. Then the first raindrops splattered against the windshield heavy, urgent drops that promised a storm far fiercer than either had expected.

Matthew's grip tightened on the wheel. "Let's find a place to pull over somewhere safe to wait it out."

Eli nodded, fingers clenched on the edge of his seat. "Yeah... that sounds like a good plan."

The Isolated Inn

A few miles down the road, Matthew spotted a small stone building tucked into the hillside—a secluded inn with a weathered wooden sign swaying in the wind. He eased the car onto the gravel lot just as the rain intensified, heavy sheets hammering the windshield with relentless force.

"Stay here," Matthew said, already unbuckling his seatbelt. "I'll run inside and see if they have a room."

Eli frowned, voice low. "You're not leaving me in the car alone."

Matthew turned, offering a half-smile that didn't quite reach his eyes. "I'm not abandoning you to the storm. I'll be right back."

Eli huffed but stayed put, gripping the door handle as Matthew dashed out into the rain. The suit jacket he'd been wearing was instantly soaked, clinging to him as he disappeared into the inn's doorway.

For minutes, all Eli could hear was the relentless drumming of rain against the roof and windshield. Then, a sharp crack of thunder rolled across the hills, making him flinch. He bit his lip, staring out at the storm, watching as the wind bent the trees unnaturally. The picturesque Tuscan landscape now felt wild and unfamiliar, almost eerie.

Just as the unease began to settle deeper, the car door swung open. Matthew was back, rain dripping from his hair and jacket. "They've got a room," he called over the storm.

Eli didn't hesitate. He grabbed their bags and slipped out, chasing after Matthew through the sheets of rain and into the warm, welcoming glow of the inn.

A Stormy Night and the 'Puff Daddy'

The inn's interior was small but cozy, with its rustic wooden beams and the warm scent of burning firewood wrapping around them like a soft blanket. A few other travelers sat near the fireplace, murmuring quietly about the sudden storm that had caught them all off guard.

Matthew and Eli climbed the narrow staircase to their room—a quaint space with a large, inviting bed, a stone fireplace, and a tiny balcony that looked out over the rain-drenched valley.

Eli dropped his bag onto a chair and shivered. "That storm came out of nowhere."

Matthew joined him at the window, his gaze scanning the relentless sheets of rain and the wind that howled through the trees. "I've been here enough times to know this isn't normal. Tuscany gets storms, sure, but they don't move this fast—or hit this hard."

Eli stepped close, his eyes following the tempest beyond the glass. "Do you think we'll be stuck here all night?"

Matthew turned with a small, teasing smirk. "Would that be so bad?"

Eli's expression softened, his voice quiet. "Not if I'm with you."

Matthew's hands found Eli's arms, warm and steady as they traced gentle lines down his skin. "Then let's make the most of it."

Downstairs, the innkeeper had laid out a small spread of treats for the stranded guests. When Matthew spotted one particular pastry, his face lit up.

"Oh my god, they have puff daddies," he said, barely able to contain his excitement.

Eli blinked. "What?"

Matthew grinned, grabbing two of the pastries and handing one to Eli. "Maritozzo—they're these sweet, airy buns filled with whipped cream. I've always called them puff daddies. Basically, heaven in pastry form."

Eli took a cautious bite, eyes widening as the delicate cream melted on his tongue. "Matthew..." He took another, slower bite, savoring it. "This might be the best thing I've ever had."

Matthew chuckled, watching Eli's delight. "I knew you'd love it."

Under the table, Eli's legs bounced with happiness as he finished the pastry. "I think I need five more of these."

Matthew laughed, reaching out to wipe a dab of cream from the corner of Eli's mouth. "You really are a walking sugar craving."

Eli giggled, leaning into Matthew's touch. "And you love that about me."

Matthew leaned in, his lips brushing softly against Eli's. "I love everything about you."

The fire crackled beside them, a comforting backdrop to the storm's wild symphony outside. Wrapped in warmth, laughter, and the lingering sweetness of puff daddies, they settled into the evening, lost in their own perfect little world.

For Matthew and Eli, this unexpected night in the storm was far from an inconvenience—it was another memory to treasure, a story woven into the tapestry of their journey together.

CHAPTER 32

A Night to Remember

The fire crackled softly in the dimly lit room, casting a golden glow across the rough stone walls. Outside, the storm showed no sign of easing—in fact, it seemed to intensify. Rain hammered relentlessly against the windows, and every so often, a fierce gust rattled the wooden shutters. But inside, wrapped in warmth and the quiet comfort of each other's presence, Matthew and Eli barely noticed the chaos beyond the glass.

Eli licked the last bit of cream from his lips, sighing with contentment. "I don't think I'll ever stop thinking about that pastry."

Matthew smirked, finishing his own maritozzo and leaning back in his chair, eyes locked on Eli. "The Puff Daddy has claimed another victim."

Eli laughed, legs bouncing slightly beneath the table. "You're such a bad influence."

Matthew arched a brow, the corner of his mouth twitching into a playful smirk. "Oh? Do I tempt you that much, Eli?" His voice lowered, smooth and warm, laced with teasing promise.

Eli swallowed hard, his cheeks flushing a delicate pink. "I—I mean, yeah. Always."

Matthew's smirk deepened as he rose from his chair, extending a hand toward Eli. "Come with me."

Eli's fingers slid into Matthew's, and he rose, heart pounding faster as he followed him toward the bed. The flickering firelight cast shifting shadows across the room, the mood quietly shifting from playful warmth to something electric, something charged with unspoken desire.

Matthew sat on the edge of the bed, tugging Eli between his legs, his hands resting on Eli's waist. "This has been the best trip of my life," he murmured, looking up at Eli, his deep brown eyes filled with nothing but adoration.

Eli softened, threading his fingers through Matthew's short hair. "Mine too."

Matthew pulled him closer, pressing a kiss against the thin fabric of Eli's shirt, just above his stomach. "I want this trip to end perfectly."

Eli exhaled, his breath catching slightly as Matthew's lips trailed upward, pressing slow, lingering kisses along his torso, his chest, his neck. Matthew's hands found Eli's waist, his fingers squeezing just enough to send a shiver down his spine.

Eli let out a soft laugh, his nerves mixing with excitement. "You're making me melt."

Matthew's voice was husky when he whispered, "Good."

With a slow, deliberate motion, Matthew guided Eli onto the bed, their bodies molding together effortlessly. The rain continued its relentless rhythm outside, but in the heat of the moment, it felt like the world had quieted just for them.

Eli's hands roamed Matthew's back, nails grazing lightly against his skin, earning a deep, satisfied hum from Matthew. Their kisses deepened, growing more desperate, more consuming. Their bodies pressed together, warmth meeting warmth, hearts pounding in sync.

The fireplace crackled. The storm raged. And Matthew and Eli lost themselves in each other.

Morning After, A Gentle Goodbye to Tuscany

The storm had passed by the time the first pale rays of morning sunlight slipped through the shutters. The room was bathed in a soft, golden haze, casting a warm glow over the tangled sheets and the two figures curled together beneath them.

Eli was the first to stir, his head resting gently against Matthew's chest. The steady rise and fall of Matthew's breath was soothing, anchoring him to the moment. He blinked slowly, adjusting to the gentle morning light before lifting his gaze to watch Matthew sleep.

For a man who always carried himself with polished confidence, Matthew looked utterly unguarded in this peaceful moment—his lips parted slightly, his features softened in sleep, one hand still resting possessively on Eli's waist as if holding him close even in dreams.

Eli smiled quietly to himself.

Matthew's breathing shifted, fingers twitching gently, before his eyes fluttered open. For a moment, he seemed disoriented, then his gaze found Eli's, and a slow, sleepy grin spread across his face.

"Good morning," Matthew murmured, his voice thick with sleep.

Eli stretched languidly, pressing a tender kiss to his jaw. "Good morning."

Matthew tightened his hold, pulling Eli closer. "We should just stay in bed all day."

Eli chuckled, nudging his nose against Matthew's. "Tempting, but we have to check out soon."

Matthew groaned dramatically. "Do we have to?"

Eli laughed softly. "Unless you want to pay for another night."

Matthew smirked, brushing a kiss against Eli's temple. "You're lucky I love you."

Eli's heart skipped a beat at those words, though Matthew had said them countless times; they never lost their meaning.

"I love you, too," Eli whispered, fingers tracing slow circles over Matthew's chest.

They lingered like that a little longer, wrapped in each other's arms, savoring the quiet stillness of their last moments in Tuscany.

One Last Taste of Italy

They left the inn late that morning, the sun shining brightly after the night's storm. The air was crisp and fresh, still carrying the faint scent of rain as they packed their bags into the car.

Matthew steered them toward a nearby village for breakfast, spotting a charming little café with outdoor tables overlooking rolling hills. The cobblestone streets shimmered with leftover rain, and the locals moved about their day as if the storm had been nothing more than a fleeting interruption.

Seated across from each other, savoring frothy cappuccinos and flaky pastries, Eli reached across the table, threading his fingers through Matthew's. "I don't want to leave."

Matthew squeezed his hand gently. "Then we'll come back."

Eli smiled, hopeful. "Promise?"

Matthew leaned in, pressing a soft kiss to Eli's knuckles. "Promise."

Their breakfast arrived just then, and Eli's eyes lit up with delight when he spotted the maritozzo pastries. He gasped dramatically, looking at Matthew as if sharing a sacred secret.

"Puff daddies!" he whispered, reverence in his voice.

Matthew chuckled, shaking his head. "I think you're officially obsessed."

Eli took a hearty bite, humming with satisfaction. "No regrets."

Matthew smirked, amused. "I'd be worried if you did."

They ate slowly, soaking in the serene morning, knowing the magic of Italy would soon be a memory—but a cherished one.

Packing Up, Looking Forward

Back at the inn, they packed their bags in comfortable silence. Every now and then, Matthew caught Eli gazing wistfully out the window, lost in thought.

Walking up behind him, Matthew slipped his arms around Eli's waist. "What are you thinking about?"

Eli sighed softly. "Just... how perfect this has been."

Matthew rested his chin gently on Eli's shoulder. "It doesn't end here. We have so many more places to see, so many more moments to share."

Eli turned in Matthew's embrace, looking up with a soft, knowing smile. "I know. But Italy will always be special."

Matthew kissed the tip of Eli's nose. "That it will."

They finished packing, checked out, loaded the car, and took one last lingering look at the sun-drenched countryside. Then, with a deep breath, they drove off toward the airport, ready to return home.

But even as Italy slipped behind them, both knew the best was still to come.

CHAPTER 33

Homecoming Fireside

The overnight flight from Florence glided into New York–JFK International Airport just before dawn. After a bleary layover marked by lukewarm coffee and the soft glow of departure boards, Matthew and Eli boarded a regional jet northward.

At 9:08 a.m., the smaller aircraft bumped and kissed the runway at Syracuse Hancock International Airport, tires screeching softly, Eli pressed his forehead against the cool plexiglass, whispering a final goodbye to his first big travel adventure.

Matthew squeezed his hand, a quiet, unspoken promise passing between them: no matter what awaited back in Willow Creek, they would face it together.

The air outside was crisp and still, a stark contrast to the warm Tuscan breeze, but as they stepped into the late morning, the comfort of "almost home" wrapped around them like a familiar blanket.

Back In Willow Creek

Late that morning, thunderheads crowned the tall maple tree on the horizon as Matthew's SUV rolled onto Sycamore Lane. Marshy heat wrapped around them like a damp quilt, thick with jasmine and brine. Neighbors had draped blue-and-white decorations between mailboxes, and someone had chalked Welcome home! Across the pavement in looping letters. The sight tightened Eli's chest with disbelief—eight months earlier, he'd arrived here with nothing but a duffel bag and a fractured heart.

Inside, the house smelled of cedar and fresh laundry. Suitcases thudded to the floor; jet lag clung to them like stubborn sand. They unpacked essentials—souvenirs from Siena, a watercolor of olive groves, three bottles of 2019 Tempranillo—before collapsing on the sofa, lulled by rain tapping the tin porch roof.

A deliberate knock cut through the hush.

Matthew rose, expecting Claire's bubbly squeal or Jenny's sarcastic greeting. Instead, the doorway was filled with a small figure dressed in black trousers, suspenders, and a broad-brimmed hat. The man's eyes were the same glacier-blue as Eli's.

"John?" Eli's mug slipped from his hand, shattering on the hardwood.

The visitor removed his hat, his voice trembling. "It's me, big brother."

Eli closed the distance in two strides. The reunion was raw—tears, laughter, apologies tangled as lightning flickered behind the curtains.

"We never stopped praying for you," John said, gripping Eli's shoulders. "Father told the community you had gone to the world, but I knew you were still out there. We sent a letter after your engagement notice," he added, voice cracking. "I slipped it into the outgoing post even though the elders forbade it. Months passed with no reply—I feared it hadn't reached you... or worse." He nodded toward Matthew. "Then a friend showed me a festival article—your face beside him." He swallowed hard. "I took every cent I'd saved, bought a bus ticket. I had to see you with my own eyes."

Matthew, misty-eyed, offered his hand. "Matthew Hawthorne."

John clasped it firmly. "Thank you for loving my brother."

"There's no giving, only sharing," Matthew replied softly.

John's expression hardened. "I can't stay. If the elders learn I came, there'll be consequences. But one of us stands with you." He pressed a folded scrap of paper into Eli's palm—an address, a phone number that that John can use every Wednesday at dusk when no one is around. "When I am ready, I will reach out."

"What about the shunning?"

"Love is heavier than their rules," John said, pulling Eli into one last fierce hug.

Rain pounded the porch roof like applause, urging them to remember every heartbeat. Then John vanished down the lane, boots splashing through puddles.

Aftershock

Eli stood trembling, the scrap of paper clenched tight in his fist. Matthew draped a fleece blanket around his shoulders and gently guided him to the couch. For several long minutes, the only sound was the steady tick of the grandfather clock.

"For years, I thought none of them cared," Eli whispered, voice cracking.

Matthew brushed a loose curl from Eli's forehead, his touch featherlight. "Your family's story isn't finished," he murmured.

A sudden flash of headlights swept across the windows—Jenny's Jeep pulling up. Moments later, she and Claire burst in, arms full of takeout dumplings and a flood of questions. One glance at Eli's blotchy cheeks froze them mid-banter.

Matthew filled them in quietly. Claire gasped, Jenny swore softly, then both wrapped Eli in a bear hug until his ribs protested.

"Family shows up in the wildest ways," Jenny said, handing him a dumpling with a small smile. "Eat. You can't grieve on an empty stomach—that's day one stuff."

They settled on the living-room rug, eating picnic-style as thunder rumbled overhead. Between bites, Eli unfolded the scrap of paper again. Beneath the address, John had penned a single verse: Perfect love casts out fear.

Midnight Visitors

The rain tapered to a drizzle as the friends left. Matthew dimmed the lights, but Eli paced restlessly, adrenaline still spiking.

Suddenly, a sharp crack shattered the quiet, glass exploding at the back of the house. Matthew sprinted toward the kitchen; Eli followed close behind. The sliding-door pane lay fractured, shards scattered around a brick resting on the floor. Attached was a cruel note: This town ain't big enough for his kind.

Matthew's heart hammered in his chest. "Aaron's friends, no doubt," he muttered, grim.

He dialed Sheriff Barnes, who sounded grim. "We get prank calls, empty threats... but this one slipped through."

Within minutes, flashing lights painted the pines blue. Deputies swept the yard; muddy boot prints led toward the canal but vanished at the water's edge. Barnes hunched over the note, jaw clenched. "Looks like Aaron stirred up more hornets than we thought. We'll post a patrol."

Eli shivered as the adrenaline finally ebbed. Matthew reached into their luggage, pulling out a bottle of Tempranillo. He uncorked it with practiced ease and poured two generous glasses.

"I wanted our first night home to be about jet-lag kisses and Tuscany stories," he said quietly.

Eli gave a wry smile. "Nothing says romance like law-enforcement floodlights."

They sank onto the hearth rug, their feet warmed by the flickering gas fire. Eli traced the stem of his wineglass, gathering courage.

"John wasn't the only one," he whispered. "I had a younger sister, Lydia. She begged me to take her when I left. I… couldn't. She was only fourteen."

The confession cracked something inside Eli, tears welling unbidden. Matthew pulled him close.

"We'll find her when the time's right," he promised gently. "That's not yours to carry alone anymore."

Dawn Resolutions

Gray light seeped through the blinds. Neither had slept. Over bold coffee from the Finger Lakes roaster, Matthew scribbled out a plan:

Security — install reinforced glass, upgrade cameras, and hire Harrison's private patrol for two weeks.

Community — create awareness of the situation.

Family — Wednesday at dusk, Eli would call the barn number.

Eli traced the plan with his finger. "You forgot step four."

Matthew looked up, curiosity softening his eyes.

"What's that?"

Eli's shy smile appeared — the one Matthew would cross oceans for. "Book our next trip. John said love weighs more than rules — I think it's braver than fear, too."

Matthew exhaled, tension easing from his shoulders. "Australia's wine country — Barossa harvest in March?"

Eli's legs bounced. "And Spain for sherry! And maybe Pennsylvania for Lydia."

Matthew laughed, kissed his tiny opal, and tasted hope beneath the fatigue.

Outside, the rain had stopped. Dawn gilded the wet street, and every puddle mirrored a new sky — clean, bright, alive.

CHAPTER 34

Night of Broken Glass

The replacement window crew pulled in at noon with crates stamped HVHZ—Hurricane Impact Rated. Each pane matched the Category 5 standards used across storm-prone Florida—a detail that made Eli's eyes light up.

"These are the same windows they use across Florida," he whispered, tracing the laminated sticker through its shipping wrap. "Nothing short of a tornado or a sledgehammer gets through. That's… actually pretty cool."

Matthew squeezed his shoulder. "If Aaron tries another brick stunt, he'll need a wrecking ball."

By dusk, only one pane gleamed where yesterday's brick had blasted through the kitchen slider, but the upgrade was worth every hour lost. Matthew signed the foreman's tablet while Harrison's private patrol SUV idled at the curb.

Despite the severity of the charges, the judge cited the lack of physical injury and Aaron's clean prior record as justification for setting bail. Community outrage flared when his uncle, a wealthy landowner, posted the bond within hours, allowing Aaron to walk free while awaiting trial.

Eli stood in the doorway, crossing his arms against the chill May wind, feeling—if not safe—at least armored in tempered Floridian resilience.

Inside, Jenny and Claire converted the dining table into a crisis hub—laptop feeds from the new cameras, Sheriff Barnes's direct line on speaker, half-finished dumplings congealing beside a pot of strong Finger Lakes coffee. The note Aaron's accomplice had hurled with the brick lay sealed in an evidence bag beneath Jenny's elbow, its jagged scrawl—This town ain't big enough for his kind—a bruise on the room's energy.

"Security step one: hurricane glass, check," Claire muttered, flipping through Harrison's invoice. "Step two is patrol scheduling. Step three—Matthew, quit pretending you're fine."

"Fine isn't the point," Matthew said, testing the new slider lock with a sharp clack. "Safe is."

Though Aaron remained in county lockup after violating bail, every creak still set Eli's nerves on edge; the sheriff had warned them about sympathetic copycats who might try to finish what he'd started.

A Spark in the Dark

At 10:17 p.m., the driveway motion sensor pinged. Harrison's guard radioed a routine perimeter sweep—no movement detected.

At 10:19 p.m., the front porch camera blinked out, replaced by static.

Matthew's phone chimed. CAMERA 1 OFFLINE.

"Generator glitch?" Jenny guessed, eyes narrowing.

"No," Eli whispered, pulse spiking. "Someone's here."

Matthew strode to the foyer, fingers tightening around the doorknob. "Claire, call Barnes. Jenny, stay with Eli."

But Eli followed, refusing to be coddled. Through the sidelights, all they saw were shadows and swaying jasmine.

Matthew cracked the door—and a smoke grenade rolled across the threshold, hissing a sulfurous cloud.

"Back!" Matthew shoved Eli toward the stairs as alarms blared through the house. Thick smoke poured into the entryway, cloaking a second crash—glass shattering in the study.

Coughing, Matthew pulled Eli toward the kitchen. Jenny grabbed Claire's sleeve, and all four tumbled onto the deck just as two Harrison patrolmen sprinted down the drive, pistols drawn.

Somewhere beyond the canal, an engine roared—then silence.

Barnes's cruiser screeched to a halt moments later. Under portable floodlights, deputies fanned out; K-9 units sniffed for accelerants.

Inside, the study window lay shattered, shards sparkling like stars across Matthew's mahogany desk—yet the kitchen slider remained intact, its hurricane lamination unscathed.

"Told you," Eli murmured, awe threading through his fear. "Florida glass."

No note this time—only a burnt-out smoke canister smoldering on the rug and, impaled on a shard, a playing card: the joker, its grin smeared crimson with spray paint.

Barnes let out a low curse. "He's taunting us."

"Or telling us he's done playing," Matthew said, voice low and steady.

Hearts Under Siege

Sheriff Barnes confirmed Aaron remained in lock-up, leading deputies to suspect the joker card was the work of a second accomplice—someone emboldened to act in his stead. The investigators wouldn't clear the scene for hours, so Matthew settled Eli beneath a porch blanket while guards reset the cameras.

Eli trembled—not from the chill, but from memories that clawed their way back: barn fires blazing under smoky skies.

"Every flame sounds the same," he murmured. "No matter the state."

Matthew cupped Eli's cheeks gently. "Look at me, tiny opal."

Blue eyes met brown; for a heartbeat, the world shrank to two heartbeats racing faster than sirens.

"We're still here," Matthew said softly. "Unbroken."

Eli's breath hitched. "If Aaron wants a war, he'll burn everything you built."

Matthew kissed his forehead, steady and sure. "Then we rebuild stronger. But we won't face him alone."

Claire stepped forward, thrusting two steaming mugs between them. "Step four," she declared—Eli's addition to their dawn plan—"was to book our next trip. I vote we book Aaron a one-way ticket to a cell instead."

Jenny cracked a shaky laugh. "Amen."

The Barn Number

Past midnight, after deputies had left and the sharp scent of spent smoke still lingered in the hallways, Matthew and Eli crouched on the study floor, carefully repairing the severed camera cables. The shattered window pane had been hastily boarded, but moonlight slipped through the cracks, casting a silvery glow over Eli's profile.

"John's scrap said Wednesday at dusk," Eli whispered, his finger tracing the joker card now sealed inside an evidence bag. "That's tomorrow."

Matthew paused, voice low. "We could postpone the call until things calm down."

Eli shook his head, determination settling in his eyes. "Love is braver than fear, remember?"

He rose slowly, shoulders squared as if bracing himself for what was to come. "We fix the cameras, get some sleep, and tomorrow I dial that barn number. If Lydia's voice answers, I want her to hear strength, not terror."

Matthew rose beside him, pride and worry etched on his face. "Then at dusk, we'll make the call—together."

Cliff Edge Dawn

At 3:04 a.m., the repaired camera feeds flickered back to life. The porch camera captured only the restless dance of maple branches in the cool night breeze. As Matthew guided Eli upstairs, Harrison's guard radioed one last discovery: barefoot footprints, small in size, traced through the canal mud. Not Aaron's.

Matthew's stomach clenched. "Someone new."

Eli squeezed his hand. "Who?"

The guard's voice was uncertain. "Prints lead to the water. Then vanish."

They climbed to the bedroom, stealing a final glance toward the dark yard. Somewhere out there, a ghost without shoes stalked the night.

Matthew locked the door, pulse hammering. Tomorrow's dusk would bring answers—or more threats. Whatever the night holds, they would face it side by side.

CHAPTER 35

Embers at Dusk

Sunlight crept across the bedroom floor like a timid cat, hesitant to disturb the two men tangled beneath the quilt. Matthew stirred first, his eyes settling on the freckled curve of Eli's shoulder, exposed where the sheets had slipped. The quiet warmth of the morning contrasted sharply with the chaos of the night before, though the faint bruise on Eli's arm was a stark reminder that danger still lingered.

Eli woke to a soft kiss pressed to the nape of his neck. "Morning already?" he murmured, voice thick with sleep.

"Barely," Matthew whispered back, husky and low. "But there's coffee downstairs and an apology croissant calling our names."

Eli rolled onto his back, the blankets sliding down to his waist. Matthew's gaze lingered on the strip of honey-gold skin now exposed. "We'll overschedule the day if we start counting 'firsts,'" Matthew said, letting the rest of the sentence dissolve into a slow, unhurried kiss, flavored with resolve and cardamom.

Eli smiled against his lips, a quiet promise in the curve of his mouth. "Then coffee first. We'll need fuel to face whatever comes next."

Matthew nodded, gently tucking a stray curl behind Eli's ear. "After that, we plan. Together."

Outside, the sun climbed higher, flooding the room with light. The world beyond held its breath, but inside, two hearts beat steadily—embers glowing softly, ready to rise again.

Slow Burn

Steam curled from the bathroom doorway minutes later, fogging the hallway mirror. Inside, water drummed a steady rhythm on tile, their laughter echoing softly off the walls. After days of fear and tension, every brush of skin felt charged—each touch doubled in its electric intensity.

Matthew pinned Eli gently against the warm wall, soap trailing rivulets over lean muscles. Eli's breath hitched as Matthew's palms traced down, memorizing every contour with reverent care.

"You're electric," Eli whispered, eyes dark and shimmering beneath dripping lashes.

"Only when I'm grounded by you." Matthew kissed the words on his mouth. The water wasn't the only thing heating up.

Hands slid, hips aligned, and the world contracted to sparking points of connection—movement that balanced comfort and yearning, a silent vow that they were alive and wholly each other.

When the water finally cooled, they surfaced, flushed and laughing. Matthew swiped away the steam from the glass. "I guess that counts as our first shower in the new, hardened-glass fortress."

"Next-level security," Eli teased, toweling off. "Rated against storms and smooch attacks."

Echoes from Home

By late afternoon, Jenny and Claire returned with lunch and an update: Sheriff Barnes had confirmed the small footprints were juvenile-sized, but no one in Aaron's immediate family matched them. Whoever had prowled the canal bank remained a mystery.

Eli tried to shove the thought aside; dusk loomed, bringing with it the barn call.

Matthew set up the sturdy landline phone.

"Ready?" he asked at 5:58 p.m.

Eli swallowed hard. "Ready."

At exactly six, the phone rang—they were calling him.

Eli's hand trembled as he lifted the receiver.

"Hello?"

A breath. Then a voice cracked with nerves: "Eli? It's Lydia. John's here too."

Eli's knees threatened to buckle. Matthew steadied him with a firm palm at the small of his back.

"Lydie... Matt... are you safe?"

Lydia's whisper spilled through the line. Their parents had forbidden her from speaking Eli's name, yet now she used it like a lifeline. She'd heard rumors—fire, exile, Aaron's arrest. She needed to know if Eli had truly found freedom.

Eli shared highlights: a job at the wine shop, love that felt like sunrise, and windows strong enough to stop a sledgehammer. He carefully skipped over the smoke grenades.

John's voice cut in, low and steady. "Dad says you can't come back. But Mom prays for you. She keeps your photo tucked in her Bible."

The words pierced Eli—painful but laced with love. His eyes shimmered.

"Tell her... tell her God walks with me here. And one day, when hearts soften, maybe the road will open both ways."

Lydia sniffled. "I found your hidden sketchbook—the drawing of Cayuga Lake. I keep it by my bed."

Eli glanced at Matthew, who mouthed tiny opal and squeezed his hand.

"Keep it safe," Eli said. "It's proof that beauty survives anywhere. Even barns. Even banishment."

A sudden bang sounded in the background—hoofbeats? A door? John's whisper sharpened. "Someone's coming. We have to go."

"I love you," Lydia breathed.

"I love you both." Eli's voice cracked as the line went dead.

He set the receiver down like fragile glass. Tears slid unchecked. Matthew caught them with gentle thumbs, then pulled Eli into a fierce embrace.

"They heard your voice. That's a bridge no one can burn," Matthew murmured.

Firelight & Wine

Night had fallen, cloaking the house in quiet shadows. Guards patrolled the perimeter while Claire and Jenny fortified the study window with plywood until the glass repair crew could return. In the backyard, embers glowed beneath a grate, warming two mugs of mulled wine—one a fruity red for Eli, the other an earthy Italian for Matthew.

Eli sat curled on Matthew's lap, wrapped in a fleece throw. The world beyond the fence felt suspended, as if caught in the hush between notes of a lullaby.

"Tell me about childhood summers," Matthew prompted, voice soft against the crackling firelight. "Something good —something not lost."

Eli smiled, fingers tracing the rim of his mug. "We'd chase fireflies. My sister believed each one carried a prayer.

If you cupped it gently and let it go, the prayer would reach heaven on a spark."

Matthew brushed a stray curl from Eli's forehead. "What did you pray for?"

"Courage. Adventure." Eli met his gaze, eyes shimmering in the fire's glow. "I think they worked."

They clinked mugs. The warmth of the wine slipped lower, pooling like liquid daring. Matthew's lips found Eli's collarbone, tasting cinnamon and clove. Eli arched into the kiss, the blanket slipping down as firelight danced in his eyes.

"Inside. Now," he whispered.

They barely made it to the stairs. Halfway up, Matthew pressed Eli against the wall, devouring soft gasps that sparked a fire louder than their racing pulses. Clothes tumbled like autumn leaves, each kiss claiming Eli, each sigh sealing a pact of body and soul.

At the crescendo—when the house itself seemed to shudder with their shared heat—Eli clung to Matthew like a lifeline, breathless laughter mingling with aftershocks.

"Pretty sure we fogged the hurricane glass," Eli panted.

"Good. Let them know what they're guarding," Matthew murmured, pressing a last kiss to Eli's temple.

Hidden Footsteps

Later, wrapped in each other and fresh sheets, they drifted into a shallow doze until the soft ping of Matthew's phone pierced the stillness.

The canal bank motion sensor. Again.

Eli tensed. Matthew reached for the device, swiping to the live feed. A small shadow flickered across the waterline, then vanished—too quick to identify.

"Not Aaron," Matthew murmured, eyes scanning the playback. "Too small. And barefoot again."

Eli's breath caught. "Maybe... John?" His voice was barely above a whisper. "He once talked about running. Escaping. During the call—I heard hoofbeats, didn't I?"

Matthew brushed a kiss into his hair. "We'll find out. We'll show Barnes the clip tomorrow. Tonight, we stay wrapped in this fortress we built."

Outside, the footprints in the mud told a quiet story—of someone drawn to light, to safety, to the pulse of something forbidden but warm.

Inside, beneath hurricane-rated glass and the hush of shared breath, two hearts—newly tethered to distant siblings, to vanished pasts—beat in calm, unbreakable cadence.

CHAPTER 36

Footprints by the Water

Dawn slipped in like a tentative apology, lavender light brushing the hurricane-rated slider. Matthew woke to the gentle hush of the canal and found Eli still curled beside him, chestnut curls splayed across the pillow in a soft act of rebellion.

On Matthew's phone, a motion sensor alert blinked amber: 07:04 A.M. Both had slept through it, exhaustion holding them until sunrise.

Quietly, Matthew slid from the bed and swiped open the security feed. His breath caught: a small, barefoot figure sat on the dock, knees hugged to their chest, staring at the water. The same silhouette from the night before.

He leaned back, heart treacherous in its rhythm. Then, carefully, he returned to Eli's side and whispered, "He's back."

A Brother by the Dock

Wrapped in a blanket, they stepped onto the deck, Harrison's patrolman trailing behind in quiet vigilance.

Dew glazed the planks like spilled glass, and the air smelled of pine, wet earth, and—for once—no smoke.

The figure on the dock turned. Eli froze.

His breath left him in a single, stunned syllable. "John?"

Barefoot, jeans cuffed above mud-slicked ankles, John —Eli's younger brother—looked older than seventeen. His eyes, red rimmed from exhaustion and something deeper, landed on Eli with a shaky kind of relief.

"Couldn't stay away," he croaked.

He wavered, voice raw from wind and silence. "Dad's sick. Really sick. The elders... they say it's your fault. That your sin brought judgment."

Eli flinched. Matthew instinctively gripped his hand, grounding himself, then stepped forward, voice gentle. "You walked all night?"

"Mostly rode a freight train out of Buffalo," John said, glancing down. "Lost my shoes crossing the river." His eyes flicked to the plywood patch over the shattered study window. "I saw the news. The fire... Aaron. I had to warn you."

Matthew didn't hesitate. He draped an arm around John's trembling shoulders, guiding him inside. The patrolman gave a curt nod and stepped back, radioing Sheriff Barnes with a calm report: Non-threat intruder. Family.

Claire and Jenny met them at the door, all questions and worried glances. Claire pressed a warm mug into John's hands. Jenny cracked open a first aid kit without a word. They didn't ask who he was. His bare feet and Eli's expression said enough.

Kitchen Confessions

An hour later, John sat at the kitchen island, both hands wrapped around a mug of hot chocolate. Eli knelt beside him, gently dabbing antiseptic onto blistered feet. The resemblance between them was undeniable—same glacier-blue eyes, though John's held more storm than sky.

"Dad's fever started last week," John said quietly. "Mom keeps praying for a sign. After Aaron got locked up again, Bishop Graber said it was righteous justice. Claimed the devil's grip had lifted from the land."

He hesitated, then added, "But Lydia... she says your happiness proves God is bigger than fences."

Eli's hands paused. His throat tightened, eyes brimming.

"I thought the bridge was burned."

John met his gaze, steady.

"It is," he said. "But bridges can be rebuilt—if someone carries the first plank."

Matthew, quiet until now, poured a bold espresso and leaned on the counter.

"What do you need, John? A safe place to land? A ride back? Or something more permanent?"

John's gaze shifted to Eli, softening. His voice was steady, but low.

"I need to see you living free. So I can decide for myself."

Sparks & Shelter

Matthew readied the guest room while Claire rummaged in Eli's closet for a spare pair of sneakers. Jenny coordinated with Harrison's team—extra eyes never hurt. By mid-afternoon, rain drummed steadily on the roof, pinning them indoors like stitches in place.

Eli found John in the study, hunched over the security monitors, his socked feet barely touching the floor.

"You okay?" Eli asked, voice low.

John didn't turn. "Not scared," he said after a pause. "Just... curious. Those windows—do they really stop bricks?"

Eli cracked a smile, leaning on the desk beside him.

"Bricks. Storms. Jealous ex-boyfriends. This house has seen it all."

A rumble of thunder rolled overhead; the lights dipped to black, then flickered back. In that heartbeat of darkness, Eli caught something raw in John's face—longing, maybe envy. A boy too young to carry exile. A brother trying to understand freedom from the inside out.

Eli rested a hand on his shoulder, gentle and firm.

"Whatever path you choose, you won't walk it alone. Not anymore."

Heat of the Moment

The storm lulled John to sleep on the couch after dinner, worn out from travel. Claire and Jenny took watch duty, joking about starting a Twilight marathon before they had to head home around 2:00 AM. That left Matthew and Eli in the hush of the study, rain tapping the plywood patch.

Eli traced the Joker card through its evidence bag. "Funny how danger and desire run on the same fuse."

"Then let's keep the lights on," Matthew murmured.

They kissed—slow at first, a rekindled promise—then quicker, urgent. Eli straddled Matthew's lap in the leather chair, thunder punctuating every gasp. Shirts vanished; fingertips mapped familiar territory. Lightning illuminated Eli's curls as Matthew's mouth found that perfect spot beneath his jaw.

The chair groaned, then tipped, sending them tumbling to the rug in breathless laughter. Matthew rolled, pinning Eli with gentle dominance. "Quiet," Eli mouthed, nodding toward the hall.

Matthew captured his lips again. "The rain's louder."

Bodies moved with exquisite friction, hips syncing to a storm-born rhythm. When the climax came—hot and shuddering—they clung to each other, rain applause on the roof.

After, breathless on the rug, Matthew brushed damp curls from Eli's forehead. "You okay?"

"Perfect," Eli whispered. "Just... perfect. "

A New Plank

Morning dawned clear, the air scrubbed clean by the storm. Sunlight slanted through the hurricane glass, painting gold stripes on the floor. Sheriff Barnes arrived before breakfast, reviewed the canal footage, and formally designated John a protected witness—shielded from retaliation by Aaron's remaining allies.

Later, Matthew drove John into town. They stopped at a secondhand shop for sneakers and grabbed coffee from the corner café. At the register, John lingered by a rack of postcards—vivid snapshots of waterfalls, rolling vineyards, and flaming autumn hills.

Matthew watched him study one in particular—Cayuga Lake at sunrise.

"Eli says you want to rebuild bridges," Matthew said softly.

John nodded, tracing the lake's mirrored sky with his thumb.

"I'm starting with one plank—right here." He tucked the postcard into his pocket after paying.

Back home, the scent of cinnamon and vanilla drifted through the open kitchen. Eli stood at the counter, curls dusted with flour like early snow, presenting a tray of cinnamon rolls with shy pride. The house smelled like sugar and possibility.

Sheriff Barnes called just after lunch. The judge had expedited Aaron's trial. Additional accomplices were being questioned. For the first time in weeks, the whole town seemed to breathe again.

Eli met Matthew's gaze across the table, hope and caution dueling in his expression.

"Maybe it's time we planned something new," he said, voice tentative. "Something... big."

Matthew reached for his hand, kissed each knuckle slowly.

"Then let's build the rest—together."

CHAPTER 37

Timbers and Truth

The next morning, sunlight spilled through the patched study window, catching motes of sawdust still suspended from the night's repairs. Claire and Jenny—relieved from their vigil—had left at first light, yawning but victorious.

John lingered by the glass, palm pressed to the hurricane-rated pane as if he could feel the safety it promised. The kind that held, even when the world outside cracked.

Downstairs, Eli whisked eggs in a ceramic bowl while Matthew flipped thick slices of cinnamon roll French toast on the griddle—an impromptu feast for three.

When they finally sat, sunlight warmed the kitchen table. John took a tentative bite, syrup soaking into the cinnamon-swirled bread. His eyes widened.

"First time I've had dessert for breakfast," he murmured, cheeks pinkening.

"You'll learn we spoil each other here," Matthew said, nudging Eli's knee beneath the table.

Eli grinned and passed the syrup again.

"And next lesson is town tour day. Sneakers on, brother —we're showing you Willow Creek's finest."

The Town Walk

Main Street buzzed with Saturday energy: merchant stalls lined the sidewalk, kids chalked wild spirals and hopscotch grids, and the rebuilt hardware storefront wore its COMING SOON banner like a badge of resilience.

Mr. Higgins waved them inside, proud and sun-dappled in the doorway.

"Whole town pitched in," he said, gesturing toward the fresh shelves rising like saplings from the sawdust floor. "Storms and arson alike—nothing breaks us for long."

John lingered at a polished two-by-four, palm tracing the grain. His thumb paused at a knot, eyes distant, as if the lumber were telling its own story.

His gaze shifted to Eli. "Bridges can be rebuilt after all," he murmured.

At the wine shop, Matthew unlocked the door for a private tasting. Cool air slipped around them, carrying hints of oak and cherry. Barrels lined the back wall like silent sentinels, steady and waiting.

Matthew poured a non-alcoholic sweet Riesling— gentle and bright—for John.

"Start here," he said, handing over the stemmed glass.

Eli set out a small plate of local cheeses, anchoring the spread with a wedge of merlot-infused cheddar.

John swirled the glass, mimicking Matthew's practiced motion. He took a tentative sip, then blinked.

"Smells and tastes like an apple."

"Good nose," Matthew said, genuinely impressed.

Eli slung an arm across his brother's shoulders, easy and warm.

"Imagine what you'll discover when we take you to the Finger Lakes vineyards someday."

John hesitated, glass cradled like a question.

"Leave the community... openly?"

Eli's voice softened to a thread of truth.

"You already did, brother. The only question is whether you'll walk back... or forward."

Courthouse Echoes

That afternoon, Sheriff Barnes called. His voice, though steady, carried the weight of consequence.

"Trial date's set—three weeks from Friday," he said. "The prosecutor wants a public show of unity. Community's strength under oath."

"I'll be there," Matthew said without hesitation.

When he ended the call, he relayed the update over late lunch. Eli reached across the table, squeezing his hand.

"We'll stand together," he said. His voice was low, certain.

From the kitchen doorway, John cleared his throat.

"If I stay... could I be there too?" His eyes flicked to Eli, then back to Matthew. "For him?"

A pause.

Matthew met his gaze, steady, but careful. "It's your choice, John."

John nodded, slow but sure. In his expression: the tremble of nerves... and the beginning of resolve.

CHAPTER 38

Hearts Unbroken

Three weeks slipped by in measured beats of preparation: sworn statements polished, evidence meticulously catalogued. Willow Creek buzzed with courtroom anticipation; every merchant storefront bore the same hand-lettered slogan in bold strokes: Justice Builds the Strongest Bridge.

Courtroom Morning

Oak benches creaked as neighbors filed into the county courthouse. Matthew sat beside Eli, their fingers interlaced, while John straightened a borrowed blazer—too broad in the shoulders, yet a perfect fit for resolve. Claire and Jenny filled the row behind them, flanking Sheriff Barnes like steadfast guardians.

Aaron entered in shackles, head lowered. A hush rippled through the room; Eli's grip tightened on Matthew's hand. But when the prosecutor called Matthew Hawthorne to the stand, a different hush settled—awed, almost reverent. Matthew's voice was steady as he recounted Aaron's threats: the smoke grenade, the harassment, the shattered glass. He never once glanced at Aaron; his eyes remained locked on Eli.

The jury returned in under an hour: guilty on all counts. A collective exhale filled the chamber. Matthew felt Eli tremble—relief mingled with a bittersweet sorrow that violence had now become a permanent part of their story.

Outside on the courthouse steps, townspeople gathered. Mr. Higgins produced a wooden plank branded with the word HOPE; children dipped brushes in bright paint, adding handprints along its length.

"For the bridge," he said, handing it to John. "You carried the first plank. Matthew and Eli told me all about it."

John's eyes glistened. "And I'm not setting it down."

Letters and Lavender

That evening, back at the house, Eli discovered a stamped envelope waiting in the mailbox—Lydia's familiar handwriting scripted across the front. Inside, a pressed sprig of lavender rested alongside a single, delicate line: When bridges are ready, we will cross.

Eli pressed the note to his chest, a quiet hope stirring in his chest. Matthew poured two glasses of deep Italian red, and one non-alcoholic red for John, handing them out with a knowing smile.

"To bridges," he said softly.

They drank slowly on the deck beneath a rising crescent moon, the night wrapping around them like a gentle promise. In the background, John strummed Claire's borrowed guitar, the soft melody weaving through the stillness. The hurricane glass slider caught their reflected silhouettes—three figures now, where once there had been only two.

Firefly Promises

Summer stretched its first true night across Willow Creek. Fireflies speckled the yard like tiny lanterns, flickering above the fresh grass. Eli chased one, laughter bright and light, then cupped it gently before releasing its glow back into the dark.

"Apple blossom wishes?" Matthew teased with a soft smile.

"Courage and adventure," Eli answered, recalling their childhood prayers and the vows exchanged beside the vineyard waterfall which was overseen by the bench on the small cliff. He turned to Matthew, eyes shimmering with the insect's faint light. "Ready for the next adventure, husband?"

Matthew slipped a hand into his pocket and pulled out a slim silver chain. At its center glowed a tiny opal, twin to the stones in their wedding bands. "A belated gift," he said, fastening it around Eli's neck. "So a piece of us stays close to your heart, wherever you go."

Eli's fingers brushed the masculine pendant, throat tightening with emotion. "I have something too." He produced a miniature bridge carved from walnut wood, the word HOPE burned across its span. "For your office—a reminder of what we've built, and what we'll keep building."

Matthew turned the carving in his hands, his voice thick with feeling. "I love it almost as much as I love you."

He drew Eli close. Around them, fireflies spiraled upward, their kiss deepening beneath the quiet night—no grand proposal needed, only the tender reaffirmation of promises already made.

Bridge of Tomorrow

Later, after the impromptu celebration had dwindled to quiet conversation and gentle guitar lullabies, Matthew and Eli lay stretched out in the yard, hands linked, eyes tracing constellations as they slowly emerged.

"Think we'll ever finish the bridge?" Eli whispered.

Matthew squeezed his fingers. "Bridges aren't really finished—they're traveled. Today we cleared the span; tomorrow we lead others across."

A shooting star etched silver across the velvet sky. Eli smiled softly. "Then let's keep walking."

They rose, heading inside through the open slider—the hurricane glass reflecting two figures framed against a horizon of endless possibility. Behind them, John carefully placed the painted plank across two sawhorses, the word HOPE glowing warm in the porch light.

Hearts unbroken, Matthew thought as he closed the door on the night—and on bridges forever growing.

About the Author

Michael Rojewski is a dedicated community leader and real estate professional based in the stunning Florida Keys. Rooted in the love and support of his family, he approaches both life and work with compassion, integrity, and purpose.

A cultured soul and avid traveler, Michael finds inspiration in the diverse places and people he meets around the world. This global perspective enriches his outlook and deepens his commitment to genuine connection and understanding.

In Hearts Unbroken, Michael shares a heartfelt story of love, courage, and the journey to find one's place—a reflection of the values that guide him every day.

Michael Rojewski